Born and raised on the Wirral Peninsula in England, **Charlotte Hawkes** is mum to two intrepid boys who love her to play building block games with them and who object loudly to the amount of time she spends on the computer. When she isn't writing—or building with blocks—she is company director for a small Anglo/French construction firm. Charlotte loves to hear from readers, and you can contact her at her website: charlotte-hawkes.com.

Also by Charlotte Hawkes

The Surgeon's Baby Surprise
A Bride to Redeem Him
The Surgeon's One-Night Baby
Christmas with Her Bodyguard
A Surgeon for the Single Mum
The Army Doc's Baby Secret

Hot Army Docs miniseries

Encounter with a Commanding Officer
Tempted by Dr Off-Limits

Discover more at millsandboon.co.uk.

UNWRAPPING THE NEUROSURGEON'S HEART

CHARLOTTE HAWKES

MILLS & BOON

First published in Great Britain 2019
by Mills & Boon, an imprint of HarperCollins*Publishers*
1 London Bridge Street, London, SE1 9GF

Large Print edition 2020

© 2019 Charlotte Hawkes

ISBN: 978-0-263-08561-7

MIX
Paper from responsible sources
FSC
www.fsc.org
FSC C007454

This book is produced from independently certified FSC™ paper to ensure responsible forest management. For more information visit www.harpercollins.co.uk/green.

Printed and bound in Great Britain
by CPI Group (UK) Ltd, Croydon, CR0 4YY

To my very first hero, who
introduced me to mountains, maths
and Marmite—love you, Dad xx

CHAPTER ONE

'ANOUK?' THE RESUS WARD'S sister poked her head around the Resus bay curtain. 'Are you running the seven-year-old casualty who fell off a climbing frame?'

'I am.' Anouk spun quickly around. 'Is she in?'

'Yes, the HEMS team are on the roof now.'

'Thanks.' Nodding grimly, Anouk turned back to her team for a final check. 'Everyone happy? Got your gear?'

The only thing she was missing was the neurosurgeon. The department had been paged ten minutes ago but they must be swamped up there. Still, she needed a neurosurgeon for the young kid. Sucking in a steadying breath, she ducked out of the bay, and slammed straight into Moorlands General's hottest commodity.

Solomon Gunn.

Six feet three of solid muscle, more suited to a Hollywood kickboxing stunt guy than the average neurosurgeon, didn't even shift under her flexing palms as the faintest hint of a woody, citrusy scent filled her nostrils.

Her skin prickled instantly. *How could it not?* It was all Anouk could do to snatch her arms down to her sides and take a step back, telling herself that the alien sensation currently rolling through her was nothing more than a basic physiological reaction.

Instinct. Nothing more.

She couldn't possibly be so unlucky as to have the Smoking Gun as the neurosurgeon on her case, could she? And, for the record, she didn't think much of the idiot who had bestowed that moniker on him. Not that it would be unlucky for the poor girl who had fallen, of course. As he was one of the up-and-coming stars of the region, the girl couldn't be in better hands than Sol's.

If only the guy weren't so devastating when it came to women who weren't in his care.

He practically revelled in his reputation as a demigod neurosurgeon and out-of-hours playboy. And still it seemed that almost every woman in the hospital wanted him.

Including, to Anouk's absolute shame, herself.

Not that she would ever, *ever* let another living soul know that fact. Solomon Gunn was the antithesis of absolutely everything she should want in a man.

Yet, caught in the rich, swirling, cognac-hued depth of his gaze, something inside her shifted and rolled deliciously, nonetheless.

She'd only been at Moorlands General for a couple of months and been in Resus when Sol had, but so far they'd never worked together on the same casualty. A traitorous part of her almost hoped that tonight was different.

'Dr Anouk Hart, I believe.'

'Yes. Are you here for my case?' Self-condemnation made her tone sharper than she might otherwise have intended.

'I don't know.' He grinned, as though he could see right through her. 'Which is your case?'

'Seven-year-old girl; climbing frame,' she bullet-pointed.

'Then I'd say you're in luck. I'm here for you.'

Her heart kicked. Anouk told herself it was frustration, nothing more.

'Lucky me,' she managed, rolling her eyes.

'Lucky both of us.'

He flicked his eyes up and down her in frank appraisal. On another man it would have appeared arrogant, maybe even lewd. But Sol wasn't *another man*; he pulled the act off in such a way that it left her body practically sizzling. An ache spearing its way right down through her until she felt it right *there*. Right between her legs.

What was the matter with her?

The man was damned near lethal.

'You might be accustomed to women throwing themselves at you.' She jerked her head over his shoulder to where a group of her colleagues was shamelessly clustered around the central desk and shooting him flirty smiles and applauding gestures. 'However, I certainly don't intend to be one of them.'

'Oh, they're just enjoying the home-made mince pies I brought in.'

'Sorry, what?'

'It *is* Christmas, Anouk.' His grin ramped up and she almost imagined she could feel those straight, white teeth against her skin. 'No need to be a Grinch.'

He couldn't have any idea quite how direct a hit his words were. She hated Christmas. It held no happy memories for her. It never had. Not that she was about to let Sol know that.

'Home-made? By whom? Your housekeeper?'

'My own fair hands.' He waggled them in her face and she tried not to notice how utterly masculine they looked. Not exactly the delicate hands people usually associated with a surgeon.

Those hands had worked magic on hundreds of patients. But it wasn't quite the same kind of magic she was imagining now.

Anouk blinked hard and tried to drag her mind back to the present.

'That's as may be, but I don't think it's your mince pies they're interested in.'

'Oh, I don't know. They're pretty good, if I do say so myself.'

'So modest.' She snorted. 'Well, if you've stopped playing *Great British Bake-Off* with your home-made mince pies...'

'"Playing *Great British Bake-Off*"?' He flashed a wolfish smile, which made her skin positively goosebump. 'I would ask if you're passive aggressive with everyone, or if it's just me, but, given the reputation you've already garnered amongst your colleagues in the few months you've been here, I fear I already know the answer.'

She shouldn't take the bait. She *mustn't*.

'And what reputation would that be?' she demanded, regretting it instantly.

His eyes gleamed mischievously. She half expected him not to answer her.

'Focussed, dedicated, a good doctor.'

'Oh.' She bit her lip. 'Well…then…thanks.'

'Even if you do walk around like you've got a stick up your behind.'

'I beg your pardon?' Heat flooded her cheeks. She could feel it.

'Sorry.' He held his hands up as though appeasing her. 'Their words, not mine. But you have to admit, you are a little bit uptight. A little *prim and proper*.'

She opened her mouth to reply, then snapped it closed again.

If she was honest, she'd heard worse about herself. At best, she was considered to be a good—even great—doctor to her patients, but cold and unapproachable to her colleagues. A bit aloof.

The only person who knew different was Saskia; her best friend since their Hollywood A-list mothers had declared each other their nemesis, over twenty-five years ago.

'Of course, *I* don't think that,' Sol continued, clearly enjoying himself. Not that she blamed him—he couldn't have any idea of her inner turmoil. 'But then, most women have a way of… melting around me.'

'How do you get away with that?' She shook her head. 'Do you actually enjoy living up to all the worst stereotypes of your own Lothario reputation?'

'Let me guess, in your book that's wrong?'

'Oh, you're incorrigible,' Anouk snapped. 'Though I assume you'll take that as a compliment.'

'You mean it wasn't?' He clasped his hand over his heart, laughing. 'I'm cut to the quick.'

A deep, rich, sinful sound, which had no right to flood through her the way it did. She hated how her body reacted to him, despite every order from her brain to do the opposite. Tipping her head back, she jutted her chin out a fraction and ignored him.

'All we know so far is that we have a seven-year-old on her way having fallen approximately nine feet off a climbing frame in a park…'

'She landed on her head and suffered loss of consciousness for a minute or so,' he concluded. 'The heli-med team are on the roof now and our response team has gone to meet them.'

'Right.' She didn't do a very good job of covering her surprise. 'So, if you could just stop making eyes at the female contingent of our team long enough to concentrate on the casualty, that would be great.'

The amusement disappeared from his face in a split second. His tone was more than a little cool.

'I *always* put my patients ahead of anything else.'

She actually felt chastened.

'Yes... I... I know that.' Anouk flicked out a tongue to moisten her lips. 'I apologise, and I take it back. Your professional reputation is faultless.'

Better than faultless. He was an esteemed neurosurgeon, rapidly heading to the top of his field.

'It's just my personal reputation that languishes in muddier waters?' he asked, apparently reading her thoughts.

But at least the smile was back, his previous disapproval seemingly forgotten. Still, Anouk was grateful when the doors at the far end of the trauma area pulled open with a hiss and the helicopter team brought their patient in.

In an instant, Anouk was across the room and

in the Resus bay, vaguely aware that Sol had fallen in quickly beside her.

'This is Isobel, she's seven years old and normally fit and well. No allergies or medications, and up to date with her jabs. Around one hour ago she was climbing on a rope basket climbing frame and was approximately nine feet up when she had an altercation with another child and fell, landing on her face or head with a loss of consciousness of perhaps one minute. She has a laceration above her left eyebrow and she has also lost two of her teeth.'

'Okay.' Anouk nodded, stepping forward. 'Thanks.'

'This is Isobel's sister, Katie.' The doctor turned to where another young girl was standing, and Anouk didn't know when Sol had moved but he was next to her. 'Katie was with her sister when she fell, and has accompanied her whilst Mum is on her way.'

Strangely, Katie lifted her head to Sol and offered a tiny, almost imperceptible shake of her head, but Anouk didn't have time to dwell on that; she needed to help her patient.

'Hi, Isobel, I'm Anouk, the doctor who is going to be looking after you. Do you remember what happened, sweetheart?' She turned to her team, who had already stepped into action. 'Two drips in, guys?'

Isobel muttered something incoherent.

'Can you open your eyes for me, Isobel?' Anouk asked, checking her young patient's pupils. 'Good, that's a good girl. Now, can you take a really big, deep breath and hold it for me?'

She palpitated the girl's chest and stomach.

'You're doing really well, sweetheart. Can you talk to me? Have you got any pain in your tummy?'

'No,' Isobel managed tearfully. 'Katie?'

'Your sister is right here, my love. We just need to check you over to see if you hurt yourself when you fell, and then she'll be able to come and talk to you.'

'Yep, got blood,' one of her team confirmed.

'Great. Okay, and let's give her two point five milligrams of morphine.' She looked back at the child. 'That will help with the pain, all right, sweetheart? Good girl.'

Quickly and efficiently Anouk and her team continued to deal with their patient, settling the girl, doing their observations, and making her as comfortable as they could. Finally, Anouk had a chance to update the girl's mum, but it was still only the sister, who couldn't have been more than ten or eleven herself, who was waiting outside the bay. Anouk remembered how Isobel had asked for Katie, and not her mum.

'Katie, isn't it?' Anouk asked softly, going over to the worried little girl and sitting on the plastic seat next to her.

The girl nodded.

'Mum isn't here yet?'

'No.' Katie shook her head before fixing Anouk with a direct gaze, her voice holding a level of maturity that set warning bells off in Anouk's head. 'But you can talk to me. I'm eleven and I can answer any questions you need me to about my sister. I'm responsible for her.'

An image of Sol and Katie exchanging a concerned look crossed her mind.

Was the girls' mum at work? Uninterested? She knew those feelings all too well. Still, she had her own protocol to follow now.

'I understand that, and you seem like a very good sister,' Anouk confirmed, standing back up. 'But I think it's better if I talk to your mum when she gets here.'

'No, wait.' Katie stood up quickly, glancing at her and then across to the team.

It took a moment for Anouk to realise that she wasn't looking at her sister so much as looking at Sol.

'You know each other?'

'I need to speak to him.' Katie nodded.

'He's just looking after your sister right now.'

'I know, he's a neurosurgeon.' The young girl clucked her tongue impatiently as though she thought Anouk was treating her like a baby. 'And you're probably going to be taking Izzy to scan her head and see if there is any damage from her fall.'

Anouk tried not to show her surprise.

'We will be.'

'Well, when he is free, Sol will come and talk to me,' Katie said confidently, but Anouk didn't miss the fear that flashed briefly in the girl's eyes.

As if sensing the moment, Sol lifted his head and looked straight at them. Then, with a quick word to one of the senior nurses in the team, he made his way over.

'You doing okay, Katie?'

Quiet, professional, compassionate. It had been

one thing to see Sol working from across a ward, to know of his reputation as a good doctor, a good neurosurgeon, but it was another actually to witness it first-hand.

Her mother had always ranted about the beauty of a brilliant actor playing a different role from the one the world was used to them adopting. That moment when the audience suddenly realised that it had forgotten who the actor was and got lost in the character.

Watching Sol at work made it almost impossible to remember his reputation as a womaniser.

And it certainly wasn't helping to smother her inconvenient crush on him.

'The doctor won't tell me anything,' Katie replied flatly.

'I'd rather explain to Mum.' Anouk bit back her irritation as Katie and Sol exchanged a glance, hating the feeling that she was missing a vital piece of information.

'Bad day?' he asked Katie simply.

She bit her lip. 'She can't even get up today. But she was resting so I thought Izzy and I could have an hour at the park before we went back and started our chores. There's no way she will be able to get here on her own.'

'I'm on call so I can't leave.' He rubbed his face thoughtfully. 'But I could call Malachi. He can help if she'd be happy about that?'

'Yes.' Katie's relief was evident. 'Please call him. I'll text Mum.'

Shifting her weight from one foot to the other, Anouk tried to control her heart, which had decided to pick up its pace as she listened to the conversation. It was aggravating feeling as though she wasn't entirely following, but the tone of it seemed all too painfully familiar. Or was she just reading too much into it?

Still, she had nowhere else to be for the moment; a nurse was with Isobel and they were waiting on a few results before they could move her to CT.

'In the meantime,' Sol's voice dragged her back to the moment, 'let me try to explain to Dr Anouk here why she can speak to you.'

Katie narrowed her eyes uncertainly.

'You're going to have to trust her,' Sol cajoled. 'I do.'

They were just words to ease the concerns of a kid, Anouk knew that, and yet she was helpless to stop a burst of...*something* from going off inside her chest.

'The more I understand, Katie, the more I can help.' She fixed her gaze on the young girl, whose penetrating stare was unsettling.

'Okay,' Katie conceded at last, before turning back to Sol. 'But you'll call Malachi?'

'Right now,' Sol confirmed.

For a moment it looked as though her face was about to crumple, the pressure of the decisions clearly getting to her. But then she pulled herself together, sinking down onto her chair and fishing out a mobile phone to begin texting. As if there wasn't time for self-indulgent emotions.

As if she was a lot older than her years with far too much adult responsibility.

Anouk fought back the wave of grief that swelled inside her. All too familiar. All too unwelcome. Coming out of nowhere.

'Anouk.'

She snapped her head up to find that Sol was beckoning her, his eyes on Katie to ensure she was preoccupied as he moved across the room.

Wordlessly, Anouk followed, letting him lead her around the curtain and into the central area, keeping his voice low.

'Katie and Isobel are young carers. They look after their mum, who suffers from multiple sclerosis. Some days are good, some not so good. Today, unfortunately, is a bad day, which means Michelle can't even get out of bed without their help.'

'I see.' Anouk breathed in as deeply and as unobtrusively as she could and tried to fight back the sense of nausea that rushed her. Her own situation had been vastly different from the girls', but the similarities were there. 'Dad?'

'Died in an RTA two years ago. He'd just popped out to get cough mixture.'

She exhaled sharply, the injustice of it scraping at her.

'Who's Malachi?'

'My brother. He'll go round and help Michelle. See if there's anything he can do to get her here. Otherwise you keep me informed throughout and we'll agree as much as we can tell Katie. She's mature, but she's still only eleven and she has enough to deal with.'

'Isn't there anyone else?' She already knew the answer, but she still had to ask. 'Any other family member?'

'No. Let me see what I can do but there are a few people I could call as a last resort. They're from the centre and they can at least sit with

Katie so that she isn't alone until my shift finishes or I can get someone to cover for me.'

'Why would you do that?' She folded her arms across her chest as though the action could somehow contain the churn of...*feelings* that were swirling inside her, so close to the surface that she was afraid they might spill out.

She wanted to pretend that it was just empathy for Katie, the familiarity of a young girl who had far too much responsibility for her tender age. But she had a feeling it was also to do with Sol. His obvious concern and care for the young girl and her sister and mother was irritatingly touching.

She was ashamed to admit that she'd been attracted enough to the man when she'd thought he was just a decent doctor but also a gargantuan playboy. Seeing this softer side to him was only making the attraction that much stronger.

'Why not do it?' He shrugged and the fact that he was clearly hiding something only made Anouk want to get to know him that much more.

It was galling, really.

Checking on little Isobel and consulting with her team was the opportunity Anouk needed to regroup, and as she worked she let the questions about Sol fall from her head, even as he worked alongside her. Her patient was her priority, as always. Soon enough it was time to take the girl to CT to scan her head and neck.

'Can I go with her and hold her hand?' asked Katie, the concern etched over her face jabbing into Anouk's heart.

She usually let parents go in to be with their child, but unnecessarily exposing an eleven-year-old to ionising radiation, however short a burst, was different.

'How about if I go in?' Sol announced over her shoulder. 'You can wait outside but I'll hold Izzy's hand for you?'

Katie eyed him slowly for a moment.

'Okay, thank you,' she conceded at length.

'Great, you walk with Anouk here and your sister. Okay?'

Something jolted in Anouk's chest at the weight of Sol's gaze on her.

'Fine with me. You're going to get leaded?'

'I thought I might. They probably won't let me in the room otherwise.'

He made it out to be a light-hearted joke, but Anouk knew better. Usually only parents were allowed to accompany their younger children into the room when the imaging was in progress.

'You don't have any patients up on Neurology?'

'I'll sort it. The only one I'm worried about right now is a Mrs Bowman, but I'll deal with that.'

The fact that Sol was putting himself into that position in lieu of the girls' mother said a lot more about him than Anouk expected.

She couldn't shake the impression that it was also more than he would normally like a colleague to know about him. Why did she feel compelled to suddenly test him?

'Boost your reputation around here to compassionate hero as well as playboy, huh?' she murmured discreetly, so only Sol heard.

He glanced at her sharply, then formed his mouth into something that most people might take to be a smile. She knew better.

'Something like that,' he agreed with deliberate cheerfulness that instantly revealed to Anouk that this was the last stunt he wanted to be pulling.

He didn't fool her. She couldn't have said how she knew it, but Sol was doing this for Isobel and for Katie, *despite* the fact that it was going to make him all the more eligible within the hospital's pool of bachelors, and not *because* of it. Which suggested there was more to Sol Gunn than she had realised.

Anouk wished fervently that the concept weren't such an appealing one.

'Right.' Shoving the knowledge from her head, she smiled brightly at Katie and then at her patient. 'Let's get you to CT, shall we, Izzy? Don't worry, your sister will be right beside you until you go in, and then again the moment you come back out.'

And that sharp jab behind her eyes as Katie slipped past her to walk next to the gurney and take her sister's hand in her own wasn't tears, Anouk told herself fiercely.

Just as she wasn't softening in her opinion of the Smoking Gun. She couldn't afford to soften, because that would surely render him more perilous than ever.

CHAPTER TWO

'WHAT'S THE STORY, *BRATIK*?'

Lost in his own thoughts, a plastic cup of cold, less than stellar vending-machine coffee cupped in his hands, Sol took a moment to regroup from the out-of-the-blue question from his big brother.

Then another to act as though he didn't know what Malachi was getting at.

'The scan revealed no evidence of any bleed on the brain and Izzy hadn't damaged her neck or broken her jaw in the fall, which we'd suspected, hence why she's been transferred to Paediatric Intensive Care. Maxillofacial are on their way to deal with the teeth in Izzy's mouth that are still loose. We have the two that came out in a plastic lunchbox someone gave to Izzy, but I think they're baby teeth so that shouldn't be too much of an issue. We won't know for sure until some of the swelling goes down.'

They had left Izzy with her mother and sister for some privacy, but, without having to exchange a word, both brothers had chosen to remain on hand. The girls' mother was going to need help, if nothing else.

'I know all that,' Malachi cut in gruffly, as though it pained him to ask. 'The paediatric doctor told me. I was asking what the story was with you, numb-nuts.'

An image of Anouk popped, unbidden, into Sol's head, but he shoved it aside.

'Don't know what you're talking about.'

It was only a partial lie.

He knew what his brother was getting at, which was surprising since they didn't *do* that *feelings* stuff, but he didn't know the answer to the question himself.

'You know exactly what I mean.' Malachi snorted. 'You forget I've practically raised you since we were kids. You can't fool me.'

Sol opened his mouth to jibe back, as he normally would. But tonight, for some inexplicable reason, the retort wouldn't come. He told himself it was the situation with Izzy. Or perhaps the fact that sitting on hard, plastic chairs, in a low-lit, deserted hospital corridor in the middle of the night, played with the mind.

He had a feeling it was more like the five-foot-seven blonde doctor who was resurrecting ghosts he'd thought long since buried. He had no idea what it was about her that so enthralled him, but she had been doing so ever since the first moment he'd met her.

It had been an evening in a nightclub where Saskia, already a doctor at Moorlands General, had brought Anouk along so that she could meet her new colleagues. The night before, he'd seen Anouk as a focussed, driven, dedicated doctor. And she'd been so uncomfortable that it had been clear that clubs definitely weren't her thing.

He'd seen her from across the room. She'd looked up and met his gaze and something unfamiliar and inexplicable had punched through him. Like a fist right to his chest. Or his gut.

If it had been any other woman he would have gone over, bought her a drink, probably spent the night with her. Uncomplicated, mutually satisfying sex between adults. What could be better? But as much as his body might have greedily wanted the pretty blonde across the room, possibly more than he'd wanted any woman, something had sounded a warning bell in his head, holding him back.

And then someone had spiked her drink—they

must have done because he'd seen her go from responsible to disorientated in the space of half a drink—and he'd found himself swooping in to play some kind of knight in shining armour, before any of her colleagues could see her.

Sol couldn't have said how he knew that would have mattered to her more than almost anything else. There was no plausible explanation for the...*connection* he'd felt with her.

So he'd alerted the manager to the situation before pushing his way across the room, grabbing the dazed Anouk's bag and coat and putting his arm around her before anyone else could see her, and leading her out of the nightclub.

Only one person had challenged him on the way out, a belligerent, narrow-eyed, spotty kid he hadn't known, who he suspected had been the one to spike Anouk's drink. It hadn't taken more than a scowl from Sol to send the kid slinking back to the shadows.

He'd got Anouk home and made sure she was settled and safely asleep in bed before he'd left her. The way he knew Saskia would have been doing if she hadn't snuck away by that point. Along with his brother. Sol had seen them leave.

Together. So wrapped up in each other that they hadn't even noticed anyone else.

He'd headed back to the club to advise them of the situation, before calling it a night; there had been a handful of women all more than willing to persuade him to stay. None of them had enticed him that night.

Or since. If he was being honest.

Not that Malachi knew that he knew any of it, of course, and he wasn't about to mention it to his big brother. Not here, anyway. Not now. Not when it included Saskia. If the pair of them had wanted him to know they'd ever got together then they wouldn't have pretended they didn't know each other back when Malachi had brought Izzy's mum up to the ward and Saskia had explained to her what was going on with the little girl.

He'd tackle Malachi about it some other time, when he could wind him up a little more about it. The way the two of them usually did.

Sol glowered into his coffee rather than meet Malachi's characteristically sharp gaze.

'I haven't forgotten anything.' He spoke quietly. 'I remember everything you went through to raise us, Mal. I know you sold your soul to the devil just to get enough money to buy food for our bellies.'

For a moment, he could feel his brother's eyes boring into him, but still Sol couldn't bring himself to look up.

'Bit melodramatic, aren't you, *bratik*?' Malachi gritted out. 'Is this about Izzy?'

'I guess.'

His second lie of the night to his brother.

'Yeah. Well,' Malachi bit out at length. 'No need to get soppy about it.'

'Right.'

Downing the last of the cold coffee and grimacing, Sol crushed the plastic cup and lobbed it into the bin across the hallway. The perfect drop shot. Malachi grunted his approval.

'You ever wondered what might have happened if we'd had a different life?' The question was out before he could stop himself. 'Not had a drug addict for a mother, or had to take care of her and keep her away from her dealer every spare minute?'

'No,' Malachi shut him down instantly. 'I don't. I don't ever think about it. It's in our past. Done. Gone.'

'What the hell kind of childhood was that for

us?' Sol continued regardless. 'Our biggest concern should have been whether we wanted an Action Man or Starship Lego for Christmas, not keeping her junkie dealer away from her.'

'Well, it wasn't. I wouldn't have asked if I'd known you were going to get maudlin on me.'

'You were eight, Mal. I was five.'

'I know how old we were,' Malachi growled. 'What's got into you, Sol? It's history. Just leave it alone.'

'Right.'

Sol pressed his lips into a grim line as the brothers lapsed back into silence. Malachi could claim their odious childhood was in the rearview mirror as much as he liked, but they both knew that if they'd really locked the door on their past then they wouldn't have founded Care to Play, their centre where young carers from the age of merely five up to sixteen could just unwind and be kids instead of responsible for a parent or a sibling.

If there had been anything like that around when he and Malachi had been kids, he liked to think it could have made a difference. Then again, he and Mal had somehow defied the odds, hadn't they?

Would the strait-laced Anouk think him less of an arrogant playboy if she knew *that* about him?

Geez, why did he even care?

Shooting to his feet abruptly, Sol shoved his hands in his pockets.

'I'm going to check on some of my patients upstairs, then I'll be back to see Izzy.'

He didn't wait for his brother to respond, but he could picture Malachi's head dip even as he strode down the corridor and through the fire door onto the stairwell.

He wasn't ready for Anouk to come bounding up the steps and, by the way she stopped dead when she saw him, she was equally startled.

'You're still here?' she faltered.

'Indeed.'

'I'd have thought you'd have gone home by now. I heard Izzy's mum arrived.'

She glanced nervously over his shoulder, as if checking no one could see them talking. He could well imagine she didn't want to be seen as the next notch on his bedpost. He almost wanted to ask her how much free time she imagined a young neurosurgeon to have that he could possibly have made time for so many women.

He bit his tongue.

What did it matter to him if she believed he was as bad as all those stories? Besides, hadn't he played up to every one of them over the years? Better people thought him a commitment-phobe than realise the truth about him.

Whatever the truth even was.

'Mal and I stayed to help.'

'Mal?'

'Malachi.'

'That's right.' She clicked her fingers. 'Your brother. You did say he was collecting the girls' mother.'

'He's through there now.' A thought occurred to him. 'With Saskia.'

'Okay.' She nodded, but her eyes stayed neutral.

Interesting. She clearly didn't know that Saskia and Malachi had had a…*thing*. He wondered what, if anything, Anouk remembered from that night. The club? The drink? The fact that he'd been the one to escort her safely home? Did she not remember him at all from that night?

'Anyway, I have to go.'

'Women waiting for you?'

That prim note in her voice had no business tingling through him like that.

'Always.'

She shot him a deprecating look and he couldn't help grinning, even as he moved to the flight of stairs, heading down two at a time.

'See you around, Anouk.'

He was briefly aware of her grunt before she yanked open the door and shot through it. Waiting a few seconds to be sure the door closed behind her, Sol turned around and headed back upstairs to the neurology department to check on his patients.

He felt somehow oddly...*deflated*.

Anouk tapped her fingers agitatedly on her electronic pad as she waited for the lift.

Why did she keep letting Solomon Gunn get under her skin? It was ignominious enough that her body was clearly attracted to him but it was so much worse that she kept wanting him to be different from the playboy cliché—*imagining* that she saw glimpses of something deeper within him, for pity's sake.

She who, of all people, should surely have known better?

She'd spent her entire childhood managing her mother. Playing the grown-up opposite her childlike mother—a woman who had perfected all the drama and diva-like tendencies of the worst kind of Hollywood star stereotypes.

She had watched the stunning Annalise Hartwood chase playboy after playboy, fellow stars and movie directors alike, convinced that she would be the one to tame them. It was the same story every time. Of course each finale was as trite as the last. Her biological father had been the worst, by all accounts, but ultimately they'd all ended up using her, hurting her, dumping her.

And Anouk had been the one who'd had to pick up the pieces and put her mother's fragile ego back together.

Not that Annalise had ever thanked her for it.

Quite the opposite.

Anouk had never quite matched up to her mother's mental image of how she should be as the daughter of a famous movie star. She'd been too gawky, too lanky; too introverted and too geeky; too book-smart and too gauche.

It had taken decades—and Saskia—for Anouk to finally realise that the problem hadn't really been her. It had been her mother.

That deathbed confession had been the most desolating moment of all. The betrayal had been inconceivable. It had laid her to waste right where she'd stood.

That was the moment she'd realised she had to get away from her old life.

She'd changed her name, her backstory, and she'd come to the UK. And Saskia, loyal and protective, had dropped everything to come with her.

In over a decade in the UK no one had come close to getting under her skin and poking away at old wounds the way Sol had somehow seemed able to do.

The lift doors *pinged* and she stepped forward in readiness. The last person she expected to see inside was the cause of her current unease. This was the very reason she'd waited for the lift instead of returning via the staircase. For a moment, she almost thought he looked as unsettled as she felt.

But that was ridiculous. Nothing ever unsettled Sol.

'Have you decided against getting in after all?' he asked dryly when she'd hovered at the doors so long that he'd been compelled to step forward and press the button to hold them. 'Anyone would think you were avoiding me.'

No, they wouldn't. Not unless he'd equally been avoiding her, surely?

Her mind began to tick over furiously. Her school teachers had called her an over-thinker as a kid. They'd made it sound like a bad thing.

'I thought you were leaving? Women to meet.'

'I am.' He shrugged casually, leaning back against the lift wall and stretching impossibly long, muscled legs in front of him.

'Up in Neurology?' she challenged.

'I forgot something.'

She eyed him thoughtfully. No coat, no bag, no laptop.

'What?'

'Sorry?'

'What did you forget?' she pushed.

'What is this?'

He laughed convincingly and anyone else might have believed him. She probably *should* believe him.

'The Inquisition?'

'You were checking on your patients,' she realised, with a start.

Who was that patient he'd mentioned earlier? Ah, yes.

'Mrs Bowman, by any chance?'

He swiftly covered his surprise.

'My patient, my responsibility,' he commented briskly.

Anouk ignored him.

'And now you're going back to support Izzy and her family.'

'Is that so?'

Her heart thundered in Anouk's chest and she didn't know if it was at the realisation of what he was doing, or the fact that she was confronting him about it.

'You play the tough guy, the playboy, but you've actually got a bit of a softer side, haven't you?'

'Vicious rumour,' he dismissed.

'I don't think so.'

The lift bumped gently as they reached the ground floor and when she swayed slightly, Sol instinctively reached out to steady her. The unexpected contact was a jolt as though she'd grabbed hold of an electrical power cable with no Faraday suit to protect her.

It coursed through her, zinging from the top of her head to the tips of her toes.

His darkening eyes and flared nostrils confirmed that she wasn't the only one who felt it.

A little unsteadily, she made her way out of the lift with no choice but to walk together across the lobby or risk making things look all the more awkward.

The doors slid open and the cool night air hit her hard. In a matter of seconds he'd be gone, across the car park and into that low, muscled vehicle of his.

Any opportunity would have evaporated. For good.

She stopped abruptly at the kerbside.

'Can I ask you something?'

'Shoot,' he invited.

She opened her mouth but her courage deserted her abruptly.

'Those mince pies the other day…were you also the one who decorated the desk with tinsel?'

He grinned.

'Sometimes in a place like this—' he bobbed his head back to the hospital '—it can be easy to forget Christmas should be a celebration. Don't underestimate how much a bit of tinsel and a few mince pies can lift the spirits.'

'Blue and white tinsel hung like an ECG tracing,' she clarified.

'Festive and atmospheric all at once.' He

grinned again, and another moment of awareness rippled over her skin.

'Right.'

'Indeed.'

They watched each other a moment longer. Neither speaking. Finally, Sol took a step forward.

'Well, goodnight, Anouk.'

'Can I ask you something else?'

He stopped and turned back to her as she drew in a deep breath.

'How is it you know this family so well? Well enough that you've saddled yourself with four of the worst shifts of the year just to get the night off to sit with those girls in there whilst your brother is helping their mum?'

A hundred witty comebacks danced on his tongue. She could practically feel them buzzing in the air around the two of them. But then he looked at her and seemed to bite them back.

'Malachi and I work with a young carers' group in town,' he heard himself saying. 'Katie and Isobel are two of about thirty kids who come to the centre.'

'So many?'

It was the bleak look in his eyes that gouged her the most.

'That's not even the half of it.' He shook his head. 'You've read the reports, probably around a quarter of a million kids are carers for a parent or other family member. All under sixteen, some as young as four or five. We want to reach them all but we've only just got the council on board. Sometimes the hardest bit is getting people to even acknowledge there's an issue.'

'*You're* raising awareness?' Her eyebrows shot up.

This really meant something to him? He truly cared?

He watched her carefully, wordless for a moment. As if he was waging some internal battle. She waited, holding her breath, although she didn't understand why.

'We're having a fundraiser on Saturday night, to throw a spotlight on the centre.'

'Solomon Gunn is throwing a charity gala?'

Something flitted across his eyes but then he grinned and offered a nonchalant shrug, and it was gone.

'What can I say? Lots of attractive, willing

women to choose from, so I guess I get to kill the two proverbial birds with one stone.'

The silence pulled tighter, tauter.

A few hours ago she would have believed that. Now she knew it was an act. And that was what terrified her the most.

Was she being open-minded and non-judgemental? Or was she simply being gullible, seeing what she wished she could see?

'Come with me.'

She had a feeling the invitation had slipped out before he could stop himself.

She frowned.

'Sorry?'

For a moment she thought he was going to laugh it off.

'Be my guest at the gala.'

Something rocked her from the inside. Like thousands of butterflies all waking up from their hibernation, and beating their wings all at once.

She had never experienced anything like it.

'Like…a date?'

'Why not?' he asked cheerfully.

As though it was no big deal to him.

It probably wasn't.

'With you?'

'Your eagerness is a real ego boost for a man, you know that?'

She aimed a sceptical look in his direction.

'I hardly think a man like you needs any more ego massages. You have women practically throwing themselves at you at every turn.'

'I'm not asking them, though, am I?' he pointed out. 'I'm asking you.'

She schooled herself not to be sucked in. Not to fall into that age-old trap. But it wasn't as easy as it had been for all those other men who had flirted with her over the years.

Because those other guys hadn't been Sol, a small voice needled her.

Anouk gritted her teeth.

'Is that why you're inviting me? Because you don't like the fact that I'm not falling over myself to flirt with you?'

'That's exactly it,' he replied, deadpan. 'I find my ego can't take the knockback.'

'Sarcastic much?' she muttered, but a small smile tugged at her mouth despite herself.

'I'll pick you up at half-past seven.'

'I might be on duty.'

'You aren't.' He shrugged.

'I beg your pardon?'

'Relax. I was just checking the rotas before and I don't remember seeing your name.'

She told herself that it meant nothing. It was pure coincidence.

'What makes you think I want to go?'

'What else are you doing that night? It's fun, and, hey, you can do something for charity at the same time.'

He was impressively convincing.

'People will think I'm just the next notch on your bedpost.'

'Some women are happy to have that accolade.'

'I am not *some* women.'

'No,' he agreed. 'You are not.'

The compliment rolled through her, making long-dormant parts of her body unfurl and stretch languidly. Her head was rapidly losing this battle with her body.

'How about this?' he suggested. 'I'll give you my ticket and you can take Saskia, or whoever you want, as your plus one.'

'You would give me your ticket?'

'Sure. That way you won't feel like I'm trying to obligate you in any way.'

'And I could take anyone?'

'Of course.'

She narrowed her eyes.

'Even a date of my own?'

'Oof!' He clutched his stomach as though she'd delivered a punch to his gut, making her laugh exactly as he'd clearly intended. 'You know where to strike a man, don't you? Yes, even a date of your own.'

'And you would miss out? On something as important to you as you've suggested these young carers are?'

'Oh, I won't miss out,' he said airily. 'I'll just go as someone else's plus one.'

It shouldn't hurt to hear. Yet it did. Anouk arranged her features into what she hoped was a neutral expression.

'Of course. You must have a whole host of potential dates just waiting for you to call.'

'So many it can become exhausting at times,' he concurred blithely.

'I'll leave the tickets behind the Resus desk for you before your shift ends tomorrow.'

And then, before she could answer, or say anything uncharacteristically stupid, Sol walked away. The way they probably both should have done ten minutes earlier.

CHAPTER THREE

'THIS PLACE IS STUNNING,' Anouk breathed as she gazed up at the huge sandstone arches that lined either side of the gala venue, and then up again to the breathtaking vaulted ceiling.

'Isn't it?' Saskia demurred.

'I feel positively shabby by comparison.'

'Well, you don't look it.' Saskia laughed and Anouk wondered if she'd imagined the tension she'd noted in her friend over the past few months. 'You look like you're sparkling, and it isn't just the new dress. Although I'm glad you let me talk you into buying it.'

'I'm glad I let you talk me into buying it, too,' admitted Anouk, smoothing her hands over the glorious fabric.

It was amazing how much confidence the dress was giving her, from its fitted body and plunging sweetheart neckline to its mermaid hemline. Three strings of jewelled, off-the-shoulder straps swished over her upper arms whilst the royal-blue colour seemed to complement her blonde hair perfectly.

'You look totally Hollywood.'

'Don't.' Anouk shuddered, knowing Saskia was the one person she could be honest with. 'I think I've had enough of Hollywood to last me a lifetime.'

'Me, too. But still, the look is good.'

'Maybe I should have been in more festive colours.' She glanced at Saskia's own, stunning emerald dress, which had looked gorgeous on the rack, but on her friend's voluptuously feminine body seemed entirely bespoke, complementing Saskia's dark skin tone to perfection.

'I look like a Christmas tree.' Her friend laughed, before waving towards the glorious eighteen-foot work of art, complete with elegant decorations, that dominated the entrance. 'Although if I looked *that* amazing I'd be happy.'

'You look even better, and you know it.' Anouk laughed. 'You've only just walked in and you've turned a dozen heads.'

'They're probably looking at you, and, either way, I don't care. Tonight, Anouk, we're going to relax and enjoy ourselves.'

'We are?'

'We are.' Saskia was firm, taking a champagne flute from the tray of a passing waiter, her beam of thanks making the poor guy fall for her instantly. 'Starting with this.'

She passed the drink to Anouk.

'You still feeling sick?' Anouk frowned.

'Yeah.' Saskia pulled a rueful face but Anouk didn't miss the flush of colour staining her cheeks.

If she hadn't known better she might have suspected that Saskia was pregnant. But that surely wasn't possible? Up until ten months ago Saskia had been engaged and, for all Saskia's confidence and effervescent personality, Anouk knew her ex-fiancé had been only the second man her friend had ever slept with.

But he hadn't been as loyal, and Anouk had never really taken to him. Whenever she'd looked at him she'd seen yet another playboy— just like her mother's lovers.

Just like Sol, a voice whispered in her head.

'Relax.' Saskia nudged her gently. 'Enjoy your drink.'

'I don't really like…' Anouk began, but her friend shushed her.

'You do tonight.'

Anouk balked.

She still wasn't sure what had happened at that nightclub. She had the vaguest memory of starting to relax and trying to have a little fun, and then a sense of panic. After that it wasn't clear, but she'd ended up back home, in her own bed, alone.

Safe.

The popping bubbles looked innocuous enough—fun, even—but all Anouk could see was her mother, downing glasses and popping pills. Had anything else passed her lips in those final few years?

'One glass doesn't make you your mother.' Saskia linked her arm through Anouk's, reading her mind.

Anouk offered a rueful smile.

'That obvious, huh?'

'Only to me. Now go on, forget about your mother and enjoy this evening. You and I both deserve a bit of time off, and, anyway, we're supporting a good cause.'

'We are, aren't we?' Anouk nodded, dipping her head and taking a tentative sip.

It wasn't as bad as she'd feared. In fact, it was actually quite pleasant. Not the cheap plonk, at least, with no bitter aftertaste. Including that of her mother.

Sighing quietly, Anouk finally felt some of the tension begin to uncoil within her.

This was going to be a good evening. She was determined to enjoy it.

'I was beginning to think you weren't coming after all.'

His voice was like a lightning bolt moving through her, pinning her to the spot. Her mouth felt suddenly dry, and even her legs gave a traitorous tremor beneath the gorgeous blue fabric.

Gathering up all her will, Anouk made herself turn around, even as Saskia was sliding her arm from Anouk's and greeting Sol as if they were good friends.

Then again, they were. Saskia had been at Moorlands General for years. Admittedly a much nicer hospital than Moorlands Royal Infirmary, where she herself had trained. Why hadn't she made the transfer sooner?

She was so wrapped up in her thoughts that she only just caught Saskia murmuring something about going to check the seating plan, too late to stop her friend from slipping away into the faceless crowd.

And just like that she was alone with Sol.

As if the couple of hundred other people in the place didn't even exist.

It should have worried Anouk more that she felt that way.

'You look…breathtaking.'

Ridiculously, the fact that he had to reach for the word, as though it was genuine and not some well-trotted-out line, sent another bolt of brilliant light through her.

And heat.

So much heat.

Which was why he had a reputation for being fatal. He was the Smoking Gun, after all.

She would do well to remember that.

'You thought I wasn't coming?' she made herself ask, tipping her head to one side in some semblance of casualness.

'I did wonder.'

Some golden liquid swirled about an expensive-looking, crystal brandy glass in his hand. But it was the bespoke suit that really snagged her attention. Expensively tailored, it showcased Sol to perfection with his broad shoulders and strong chest, tapering to an athletic waist. The crisp white shirt with the bow tie that was already just a fraction too loose suggested a hint of debauchery, as though he was already on the brink of indulging where he shouldn't.

With her?

She went hot, then cold, then hot again at the thought. It was shameful that the idea should appeal so much. The simmering heat seemed to make her insides expand until she feared her flesh and bones wouldn't be able to contain her. He was simply too...*much.*

He isn't your type, she told herself forcefully. Only it didn't seem as though her body wanted to listen.

'I thought perhaps I could introduce you to some people.'

'Oh.' That surprised her. 'Is that why you came over, then?'

He hesitated, and then offered a grin that she supposed was meant to look rueful but just looked deliciously wicked instead.

'Not really.' He made it sound like a confession yet he deliberately didn't elaborate and Anouk wasn't about to play into his hands by asking him.

'I see,' she lied.

'Do you indeed?' he murmured. 'Then perhaps you might explain to me why I couldn't resist coming over here the instant I saw you walk in.'

Her chest kicked. Hard. It didn't matter how many times she silently chanted that he couldn't affect her, Anouk realised all too quickly that she was fighting a losing battle. She had no idea how she managed to inject a disparaging note into her voice.

'Does that line usually work?'

'I don't know, I've never used it before. I'll tell you next time I try.'

She bit her tongue to stop herself from asking when that next time would be. He was clearly baiting her, but what bothered her was that it was working.

'Besides…' his eyes skimmed her in frank, male appreciation, and everywhere his eyes moved she was sure she nearly scorched in response '…if I hadn't come over then some other bloke would have. You're much too alluring in that gown.'

'But not out of it?' she quipped.

His eyes gleamed black, his smile all the more wolfish. Too late, Anouk realised what she'd said.

'Is that an invitation? I have a feeling I would be breaking quite a few harassment in the workplace rules if I admitted to imagining you out of that dress.'

'I mean… I didn't mean… That isn't what I intended.'

'Then be careful what you say, *zolotse*, you can build a man up too quickly otherwise.'

'*Zolotse?*' she echoed. It sounded… Russian, maybe?

'*Zolotse,*' he confirmed.

It was the way his voice softened on that word—as if he hardly knew what he was saying himself as he moved closer, his body so tantalisingly close to hers and his breath brushing her neck—that sent a fresh awareness singing through her veins. It made her forget even to draw breath.

Her mind struggled to stay in control.

'You don't intend to elucidate?' She barely recognised her own voice, it was so laced with desire.

'I do not,' he muttered.

Now that she thought about it, Sol and Malachi both had a bit of a Russian look about them. But if they were Russian then it was something

Sol didn't share with many other people. Certainly it wasn't common knowledge around the hospital.

Which only made her feel that much more unique.

Dammit, but the man was positively lethal.

Three hours had passed since she'd arrived.

Three hours!

It felt like a mere five minutes, and all because she'd been in Sol's company.

The man had turned out to be a revelation. She'd known he was intelligent, witty, devastatingly attractive, of course. The whole hospital talked about him often enough. But knowing it and *experiencing* it turned out to be two entirely different things.

He had a way of making her feel…special. And it didn't matter how many times she cautioned herself that this was his trick, every time he stared at her as though she were the only person in the entire room, an incredible thrill skewered her like a javelin hurtling through her body.

Even as he'd introduced her around the room— to contacts to whom many of the top consultants would have amputated their own limbs to be introduced—she'd had to fight to concentrate on what he was saying. The feel of his hand at the small of her back kept sending her brain into a tailspin.

She felt like a reed, bending and turning, twisting wherever the breeze took her, and right now that breeze took the form of Solomon Gunn. He was swaying her at will and yet all he was really doing was moving smoothly through the throng, his hand barely touching her searing flesh.

Still, she smiled and greeted and charmed, just as she'd learned to do at the knee of her Hollywood mother. And she made no objection to what Sol was doing.

Perhaps because a portion of her longed to wallow shamelessly in the glances cast their way?

Some admiringly. Others enviously. She'd been on the receiving end of enough sugar-coated scowls and underhanded digs to know that she wasn't the only one to have noticed Sol's attention to her. Or realise that this was more than just his usual behaviour towards a woman on his arm.

He was giving her his undivided attention and presenting her as though she were a proper date.

Half of the room seemed to be more than conscious of his body standing so close to hers. As though she were more than just a colleague.

As though there were something intimate between them.

And yet she couldn't bring herself to care the way she suspected she might have cared a few days ago.

His gentleness and compassion with the young family the other night still played on her mind.

Sol might be renowned for caring about his patients, but she'd seen the way he'd stayed with that family even when he was off duty, helping the girls' mother even when he should have been getting much-needed rest.

Too natural, too easy. A world away from the playboy Lothario she'd once thought him to be. It fired her curiosity until she couldn't ignore it any longer.

'I must say that, whilst I don't know your brother all that well, I wouldn't have thought a gala ball to raise money for kids was something you'd be interested in. Let alone quite so heavily involved with. It begs the question of *why*.'

'If there is something you want to know, then

ask. I am an open book, *zolotse*.' He shrugged breezily, and yet it tugged at Anouk.

Was there more going on behind his words than Sol was willing to reveal?

It was all she could do to stay brisk.

'Next you'll be telling me that you're misunderstood. That your playboy reputation is a terrible exaggeration.'

Was she really teasing him now?

'On the contrary.' He shook his head, his stunning smile cracking her chest and making her heart skip a beat or ten. 'My reputation is something for which I've never made any apologies.'

'You're proud of it,' she realised abruptly.

And there was no reason for the sharp stab of disappointment that lanced through her at that moment. No reason at all.

'I wouldn't say I was proud of it, but then I'm not ashamed of it either.'

His nonchalance was clear. She had only imagined there was another side to him because that was what she'd wanted to see. What her mother had always done with her own lovers.

It galled Anouk to realise that she was more like her mother than she'd ever wanted to admit.

'Perhaps you should be ashamed of it,' she

challenged pointedly, but Sol simply flashed an even wider, heart-thumping grin.

'Perhaps. But you could argue that I'm better than many people because I'm above board. I don't pretend to be emotionally available and looking for a relationship to get a woman into bed, only to turn around and ghost her, or whatever.'

'No, but women practically throw themselves at your feet and you sleep with them anyway.'

'They're grown women, Anouk, it's *their* choice.'

Anouk snorted rather indelicately.

'You must know they're secretly hoping for more.'

'Some, maybe. But I make no false pretences. Why does this rile you so much, Anouk?' His voice softened suddenly. 'Is this about what happened with Saskia? Or did some bloke treat you that badly in the past?'

He might as well have doused her with a bucket of icy water.

What was she doing arguing with him about this? Letting him see how much it bothered her just as clearly as if she'd slid her heart onto her sleeve.

She fought to regroup. To plaster a smile on her face as though she weren't in the least bothered by the turn of conversation. But she feared it looked more like a grimace.

'No, I'm fortunate that I've never been treated that way.'

She didn't add that she'd watched her mother repeat the same mistake over and over enough times never to be caught out like that.

'Never?'

'Never,' she confirmed adamantly.

As though that would rewind the clock. Back to the start of the conversation when she hadn't been quite so revealing about herself. Or the start of the night before she'd let Saskia walk away and leave her alone with him. Or three days ago when they'd worked together on little Isobel and she'd arrogantly imagined she saw something in the man that no one else appeared to have noticed.

The worst of it was that there was some component of her that didn't want to rewind anything. Which, despite every grey cell in her brain screaming at her not to be such an idiot, was enjoying tonight. With Sol.

'In that case, there's something else you should

bear in mind.' He leaned into her ear, his breath tickling her skin, and it was like a huge hand stealing into her chest and closing around her heart. 'There are plenty of women who enjoy no-strings sex just as much as I do.'

Don't imagine him in bed. Don't.

But it was too late.

Anouk wrinkled her nose in self-disgust.

'I get that in your twenties, but you're—what? Mid-thirties? Don't you think you might want to grow up some time? Settle down. Be an adult.' She cocked an eyebrow. 'You aren't Peter Pan.'

'That's a shame, because you'd make the perfect Tinker Bell.'

'I'm not a ruddy fairy,' she huffed crossly.

'See?' he teased, oblivious to the eddies now churning within her. 'You even have the Tinker Bell temper down flawlessly. Clearly we're perfectly matched.'

'We most certainly are not,' she gasped.

And he laughed whilst she pretended to be irritated, even though she still didn't try to pull away. So when Sol's hand didn't leave her, when his body remained so close to hers without actually invading her space or making her feel crowded in, and when he deftly steered her out of the path of a couple of rather glassy-eyed, lustful-looking men, she found it all such an intoxicating experience.

As though Sol wanted to keep her to himself.

No, she was being fanciful, not to mention ridiculous.

And still that knot sat there, in the pit of her stomach. Not *apprehension* so much as…anticipation. She was waiting for Sol to do something. More than that, she *wanted* him to.

Perhaps that was why, when reality cut harshly into the dream that the night had become, Anouk was caught completely off guard.

'Now, these are the Hintons,' he leaned in to whisper in her ear as a rather glamorous older-looking couple approached. 'She was a human rights lawyer whilst he was a top cardiothoracic surgeon. They're nice, too.'

'How lovely to meet you.' The older woman smiled at her, but her old eyes burned brightly as they looked her over thoughtfully. 'Anouk Hart… Hartwood… Hmm. You seem familiar, my dear?'

'No, I don't think so.' Anouk forced herself to smile back but her cheeks felt too frozen, her smile too false.

The woman peered closer and Anouk could feel the blood starting to drag through her veins even as her heart kicked with the effort of getting it moving again.

'Yes, definitely familiar.' She nudged her husband, who was still beaming at Anouk. 'Don't you think so, Jonathon?'

He pondered the question for a moment.

Anouk tried not to tense, not to react, but she could feel herself sway slightly. Not so much that a casual observer might notice, but enough that a man standing with his hand on her back might. Certainly enough that Sol did.

His head turned to look at her but she kept staring straight ahead, a tight smile straining her lips.

'Around the hospital, no doubt.' She had no idea how she injected that note of buoyancy into her voice. 'Or maybe I just have one of those faces.'

'Oh, no, my dear, you do not have *one of those faces.*' The woman chuckled.

'More like a screen icon,' her husband agreed, then his face cleared and Anouk's stomach plummeted. 'Like Annalise Hartwood.'

'Annalise Hartwood,' the woman echoed delightedly. 'And she had a daughter…what was her name, Jonathon? Was it Noukie?'

How she'd always hated that nickname. She was sure her mother had known it, too. It was why Annalise had used it all the more.

'Noukie…' He nodded slowly. 'Yes, I think it might have been. You're Noukie Hartwood.'

As if she didn't already know! They said it as if it were a nugget of gold, a little bit of information that they were giving her.

Anouk wanted to shout and bellow. Instead, she stood exactly where she was, her smile not slipping, muscles not twitching.

'Anouk Hart.' She tried to smile. 'Yes.'

'My goodness, I can hardly believe it. Annalise was such a screen icon in my day. But, my dear, you don't have any American accent at all, do you? How long have you been over here?'

How it hurt to keep smiling.

'My friend and I came to university over here…' she paused as if she were searching for the memory, when the truth was she knew practically to the week, the day '…so a little over ten years ago.'

The moment her mother had died and Anouk

had finally felt free of her. What kind of person did that make her?

But then, after her mother's deathbed revelation, who could blame her? To realise that her mother, her grandmother, had been lying to her about her father for eighteen years.

What kind of people did that make *them*?

'It was awful what happened to your mother, dear. God rest her soul.'

Their sympathy was apparent, but all Anouk could feel was how relieved she'd been. It had been awful, but it had also been liberating.

What had felt awful had been getting to the UK, tracking down her father from an address on a fragment of paper, only to discover that he had died a few years earlier. Her eyes pricked, hot and painful, at the memory. It had been the moment she'd realised the truth had been buried from her, quite literally if she thought about it, for ever.

She hastily blinked away the inconvenient tears. This was no time for sentimental nonsense. Sol's eyes were boring into her. Seeing her in a new way. Or maybe seeing her in the old way, the way she hadn't wanted anyone to look at her ever again.

'Yes, well...' The smile was as rigid as ever but suddenly she felt like a sad, lonely, frightened kid all over again.

You are a successful doctor, she chanted silently to herself. *Successful*. That wasn't her life any more.

'I know it wasn't public knowledge, my dear. But we knew of the rumours. The things you did for her.'

'No... I...' The practised denial was on her lips but it had been so long. So many years.

'What a marvellous ambassador for the young carers you will be.' The woman brightened up, and it took Anouk a moment to realise what she was implying.

She opened her mouth to interject but the woman was already turning to her husband.

'Noukie, here, will make a wonderful role model. Don't you think, Jonathon?'

'Oh, quite, quite,' he agreed solemnly, completely oblivious of the turmoil their observations were churning within Anouk. 'Letting them know it doesn't matter what your background—even the glitz of Hollywood—being responsible for someone else, like a parent, can happen to anyone.'

She couldn't focus. They were still talking but the words were becoming more and more distant and muffled. Her brain was shutting down despite her attempts to fight it. She tried to tell them that they had it all wrong, that she wasn't anyone's role model, but they were caught up in their excitement and weren't listening.

She wasn't really aware of Sol taking charge, winding the conversation up in a natural, easy way, but she knew he must have done, because the next thing she knew he was guiding her gently but firmly through the crowds without commotion. Or, certainly, no one seemed to be paying her any more or less attention than they had been before.

It was only when she found herself in a quiet anteroom that she felt herself starting to come to.

CHAPTER FOUR

'SORRY.' SHE BARED her teeth in what she desperately hoped would pass for a wide smile. Her stiff cheeks screamed in protest. 'Don't know what happened there.'

'I think you do.'

It was soft, compassionate even. Something pulled, like a painful band, in her chest. She could deny it, but what would be the point?

'So, Noukie Hartwood? I never knew.'

She really didn't want to answer and yet she found herself speaking. Why was it so much easier to talk to Sol?

'I always hated Noukie,' she managed.

'And the surname?'

She lifted her shoulders.

'I shortened it to Hart when I came to the UK.'

'Why?'

'I don't know.' That was a lie. 'To put some distance between myself and my mother, I guess.'

'Because she'd died?'

'She took an overdose,' Anouk clarified brusquely as she shot him a sharp look. 'I thought everyone knew that.'

'I'm aware of the story,' he acknowledged after a moment.

There was no need for her to say anything else, and yet she found herself speaking, her voice high and harsh.

'Of course, she probably didn't mean to. She had a new movie coming out and I think it was her attempt at a publicity stunt gone wrong. That's who she was.'

She could practically feel the emotions dancing inside her. Or stomping inside her. Not that it made much difference; either way, they were having a field day.

What was she doing, bleating on?

'Anyway.' She shook her head back, straightening her shoulders. As if that could somehow make her feel stronger. 'I don't want to talk about this any longer.'

Whatever she'd expected him to say, it wasn't the quiet observation that he came out with.

'No one ever does, which is part of the problem. Why do you think we're here tonight, Anouk? At this obscenely lavish ball, which costs so much per head that we could probably fund a young carers' centre for a year?'

'Maybe because people have cared enough to come out?' she bit back.

'No, because too many people as rich as most of the guests here tonight would rather throw money at an issue and get back to enjoying themselves guilt-free, than actually look at a problem and talk about it.'

She couldn't say what it was about his tone that made her ears prick up.

'That sounds remarkably like someone who has come from nothing and been on the wrong side of those issues.' She eyed him curiously, glad of the opportunity to set her own personal problems aside for a moment. 'I thought you and Malachi were millionaires? Family money or something?'

'You're changing the subject.'

'And you're evading my question,' she countered.

He contemplated her for a long minute. The band was pulling tighter around her chest with each passing second. So tight that she could barely breathe. Anouk swung around, forcing one leg in front of the other, until she found herself by an exquisitely carved writing desk with a stunning leather inlay.

She reached out to pick up an unusual-looking paperweight as if it could distract her mind, and pretended to herself that her hands weren't shaking.

'I'm not changing the subject, I just don't want to discuss it. I put that chunk of my life behind me a long time ago.'

'If that were true then you wouldn't have gone so white in that ballroom that I feared you were about to keel over. Besides, you don't just lock it away and pretend it doesn't exist. It informs what you do in later life. It's why you're a doctor now.'

She hated that he sounded so logical.

'You think you know me so well,' she threw at him caustically.

'So tell me I'm wrong.'

The worst of it was that they both knew she couldn't do that. So, instead, she spluttered a little.

'Because of course, of all people, you'd understand.'

'More than you'd think.' His voice was still impossibly even whilst she felt scraped raw.

'Then *you* talk.'

'I'm not the one who is struggling right now.'

It was odd, but the more empathetic he sounded, the more she wanted to throw the damn paperweight at his head. Carefully, she used her free hand to prise it out of her clamped fingers and set it back down before turning around. Her teeth hurt from clenching them so she struggled to loosen her jaw, too.

'You think you can help me?' she managed testily.

'Maybe…' he shrugged '…but more likely just talking about it will allow you to help yourself.'

'It was a lifetime ago. It's dead and buried.' She jutted her chin out stubbornly, hoping her whole body wasn't shaking as much as she feared it was.

'I told you, it doesn't work that way. Don't underestimate the monsters inside, Anouk. They exist. They're real. They know where your vulnerable spots are and they know just when to hit you for maximum effect. If you can't even admit they are there, how will you ever defeat them?'

'That's the sort of thing I imagine you say to your patients. Do you really believe that? Have you ever actually practised what you preach, Sol?'

'I've never needed to.' His voice raked over her skin. 'I'm fortunate that my life has been… uneventful.'

She narrowed her eyes, trying to decide whether he was telling the truth. Something in her whispered that he wasn't but he looked so easy, so calm, that she thought she might be wrong. So if he *was* deceiving her then he had to be one of the most convincing liars in the world.

She wasn't sure which truth disappointed her the most.

She stared at him, not trusting herself. She hadn't talked about this in over a decade. The only person who knew the truth—or at least, the sanitised, abridged version—was Saskia.

Solomon Gunn should be the last person in the world she would *ever* talk to about her past. And yet there was a crazy part of her that wanted to open up and spill out every last truth. Right here, right now.

'The term is *confront to get closure*,' he added nonchalantly.

She wanted to gouge that part of her out with the letter opener lying on the desk behind her. And she hated that she felt this way. So out of control.

'The term—' she narrowed her eyes '—is *sod off*.'

He watched her for a moment, his eyes so intense that she had to drop her gaze to his mouth to protect herself from plunging right into them.

'You know it's funny, everyone says you're this gentle, sweet-natured, conservative person. They obviously don't see this other side of you, but I do. Why is that?'

She felt as if she'd been caught with her hand in the proverbial cookie jar. Her heart pounded loudly in her chest and all she could do was be thankful that he couldn't hear it.

'You don't know what you're talking about.' She was impressed at quite how haughty she managed to sound.

Sol, it seemed, was more amused than intimidated.

'Oh, trust me, I do. I know women well enough. I seem to push all your buttons, Anouk Hart.'

'You wouldn't know my buttons if I waved them in your face,' she retorted, congratulating herself on her quick wit.

It was only when he laughed—a deliciously rude and decidedly dirty sound—that she realised quite what she'd said.

Again.

'I do admire a good double entendre. First the invitation to get you out of that dress, and now this. I would say that I believe your subconscious is trying to tell you something, Anouk. But I see you've cleverly managed to manipulate the subject after all.'

'There is a silver lining, then,' she managed, perching on the edge of the desk, her legs stretched in front of her, her arms extended either side of her with her hands resting on the polished wood, too.

It had been a move intended to show she wasn't as cornered as she felt, but she hadn't been prepared for Sol's reaction.

His eyes dropped down her body, as though taking in every new curve she had inadvertently revealed, from the deep plunge of her dress to the way the fabric clung to her thighs. Even the skyscraper heels that she had borrowed from Saskia.

She folded her arms over her chest, realising too late how it made her cleavage appear to swell and threaten to spill over the glorious blue fabric. But then she saw the effect it was having on Sol and her entire body burned.

It was thrilling, the way his eyes raked over her as though he couldn't tear his gaze from her. As though he ached to do so much more than simply look.

It was empowering, too.

Anouk didn't think—she couldn't afford to talk herself out of testing her theory—she just acted. And so what if she didn't believe it when she told herself that all she was trying to do was prevent him from asking any more questions?

Pushing herself up from the desk, she stood and faced him, and Sol didn't miss a moment. His eyes turned molten, his body—all six-foot-three of broad-shouldered, sculpted, wholly masculine beauty—looked suddenly taut and the room started practically humming with sexual tension.

The silence in the room was almost deafening.

Had she ever felt so desired? So confident? So reckless?

'Are you seducing me?' he demanded, the hoarseness of his tone making her blood actually tingle in her veins. 'Because if you are, I can tell you that you're going to need to be a little more persuasive.'

He was lying and they both knew it.

'That can be arranged,' she murmured before her brain even seemed to have kicked into gear.

It was as though someone completely separate to her had taken control of her body, a confident, sexually assertive persona that she herself had never felt in her life before.

It was exhilarating.

With exaggerated care, she reached around and unzipped the low back of the dress.

'What are you doing, Anouk? This isn't you.'

Another hit of triumph punched through her at the slightly raspy tone to his usually rich timbre.

'I'm shutting down any more of your conversations about my past, in the only way I know you'll respond to,' she replied, shocked at how controlled her voice sounded when inside it felt as if a thousand fizzing fireworks were all going off at once.

'I thought you told me you were only coming tonight on the premise that it wasn't a date, and that you wouldn't be sleeping with me?' he bit out, but she could see him clenching his fists at his sides.

As if he was trying so desperately to keep himself in place and maintain that distance between them. Her heart hammered in her chest, every fibre of her body on edge.

'Oh, believe me, I have no intention of either of us doing any *sleeping*.'

She could see him, coiled and ready. Just about holding himself in place.

'This isn't who you are, or what you do, Anouk,' he growled. 'I'm trying to be a good man here, but there's a limit to how far you can push me.'

'So this isn't what you wanted tonight?' She flicked a tongue out over her dry lips.

She had expected him to break by now and seduction wasn't really one of her skills. How did she convince him that she wanted this, too?

'I'm sick of playing the good girl,' she bit out. 'The responsible girl.'

Noukie Hartwood, the reliable, responsible, *boring* child of the amazing Annalise. Tedious, joyless, a killjoy. And all the other words her mother had flung at her throughout her childhood that had suggested that she didn't have a fun, daring, spontaneous bone in her body.

'Maybe I've decided it's time I had a bit of fun.' She shrugged, almost starting when her dress slipped and threatened to expose her completely, but just about catching herself in time. 'With you.'

'Consider this your last warning, Anouk,' he growled, his gaze riveted on her gaping bodice.

With a final grasp of that confidence she seemed to have acquired for one night only, Anouk shimmied and let her dress slide gracefully down her body to puddle at her feet. She had no idea how she managed to make her legs move enough to step elegantly out of the pool of blue fabric, her eyes locked with Sol's.

'Duly considered,' she murmured.

He moved so fast she was barely aware of it, crossing the space between them to haul her to him.

'Don't say I didn't warn you, *zolotse*,' he growled.

And then suddenly his lips were on hers, only for a fraction of a second, brushing them softly, almost as if he was testing her. It was startling, and it was dangerous, not least because it didn't unsettle her so much as thrill her. Yet still she didn't pull away, not even when he laced his fingers through her hair, met her unblinking gaze again and held it as he slowly—torturously slowly—lowered his mouth to hers and everything…*shifted.*

It wasn't just a kiss. Or, at least, it wasn't like any kiss Anouk had ever known before. It was the most powerful, intense, head-rush kiss that she had ever believed possible. He was claiming her, teasing her, torturing her. There was something so primal, so raw in his tone that every thought melted out of Anouk's head and it seemed to go on for ever. Dipping and tasting, scraping and teasing. Electrifying her like nothing Anouk had ever experienced before.

But then, *Sol* was like no one she had ever kissed before. With every slide of his lips, hunger seared through her, white-hot, torrid. With every sweep of his tongue she was rent apart. With every graze of his teeth she struggled to control a slew of fracturing sensations, too many to contain. *Too much.*

With each drugging drag of his mouth, and every divinely wicked slide of his tongue, he detonated something inside her. Over and over. Until he angled his head for a better, deeper fit, his hands dropping down her back, skimming the skin, tracing her sides, spanning her lower chest, just under her breasts.

It was how she imagined an initial bump of ketamine would feel, giving her a sudden head rush, making her feel giddy and fluffy. And yet, inconsistently, she was also entirely too aware of herself.

Too hot. Too jumpy. Too *everything*.

He drew whorls on her bare skin, leaving the rest of her body resenting the material that barred him from drawing them everywhere else. And when he returned to cup her face, her entire body ached for him.

Sol was *too much*. And yet she simultaneously couldn't get enough. She placed her hands on his chest as if to anchor herself, realising too late her mistake. The solid wall of warm steel beneath her palms only served to detonate even more fireworks within her. It was impossible to stop her fingers from inching across, exploring and acquainting herself with all the care that her old grandmother used to take reading her braille books. Anouk's imagination filled in all the blanks of the utterly masculine body that lay beneath the slick, tailored suit. Every ridge, dip, and contour. In stunningly vivid technicolour.

How she longed to see it for herself. She felt helpless, and aching, and desperate. Her body entirely spring-loaded with a kind of wanton desire.

When had sex ever been quite like this? So charged, so full of expectation and need? She didn't have an abundance of experience, it was true; but she wasn't exactly an untried virgin, either.

Without quite knowing what she was doing, Anouk flattened her body to his, crushing her suddenly heavy breasts to his chest as though it might afford them some relief. And then Sol let one hand glide down her collarbone, over her chest, and all he did was gently graze one thumb pad over a straining peak and pleasure jolted through her as if he'd just shocked her.

She arched into him, a silent plea for more. She couldn't seem to get close enough. Perhaps she couldn't.

'If you carry on like that, we're not going to stop,' he warned, his mouth barely breaking from hers and yet she felt the loss acutely.

Looping her arms around his neck, Anouk pressed herself closer to him. If she was going to do something so outrageously out of character, then she was going to enjoy every single second of it.

'Promises, promises,' she muttered.

'Not a promise,' rasped Sol. 'Fair warning.'

'Warning taken,' she muttered, her lips tingling as his mouth continued to brush her. 'Now you just need to prove it.'

It was insanity.

Not the fact that he was in a side room at a party with a beautiful, practically naked woman in his arms—he shamefully had to admit this had happened many times in the past—but rather, the insanity was that he was here with Anouk and she was making him feel more out of control than he'd ever felt with anyone else.

As though he couldn't have resisted her inexperienced seduction even if he'd wanted to. As if she had that kind of power over him. Which, of course, was sheer nonsense.

But he wasn't about to put it to the test and try to pull away from her now. Not when his whole body was igniting at the feel of her smooth, silky skin and scraps of lace beneath his palms; the taste of her skin on his lips and tongue; the way she shivered so deliciously when he grazed his teeth down that long line of her neck.

Not to mention that sinful garter belt, which he really hadn't been expecting from prim Dr Hart. Did he take it off her, or leave it on?

His head couldn't keep track of all the ways he wanted this woman. He wanted her with an intensity, a fierceness that almost floored him. He thought it might kill him and he couldn't even bring himself to care. As long as he had her.

Lowering his head, he claimed her mouth again and again, tasting her with his lips and his tongue, whilst she met him stroke for stroke. He captured each one of her soft sighs in his mouth, emitted as though she was as driven by desire as he was.

He let his hands trail over her body, revelling in the way her body quivered beneath his touch, and every time she pressed herself against him. He relished the way she lifted her hands to fumble with his shirt buttons and then slid them inside to trace the ridges of his chest as if she was trying to commit them to memory merely by touch.

He didn't even remember when he'd lost his jacket or bowtie. When he'd begun to cup that peachy backside to lift her up to sit on the desk, her hard nipples raking over his chest, his hips locked within the tight embrace of her incredible long, slender legs.

He was so hard, so ready he could barely think straight. *Barely.* But he could think enough to register that if she rocked against him much longer then he was going to be beyond help.

'Are you on the pill?' he muttered.

'Hmm?' She lifted her head to meet his gaze, her eyes glazed and overflowing with naked desire so that it was almost his undoing.

'I don't have any protection on me.' Every word felt as though it was being torn from Sol's throat, especially when he wouldn't have slept with any other woman without protection yet all he could think about with Anouk was burying himself deep inside her and driving them both to oblivion.

It made no sense.

'Oh.'

She flushed, and he couldn't help himself lowering his head and following the pretty flush with his lips.

She moaned softly and it went straight to his sex as surely as if she'd gripped him with her hands.

What the hell had he been saying?

'Protection,' he remembered hoarsely.

Another brief pause and then she shook her head.

'Oh, Lord…no. No pill.'

She loosened her legs from around his hips as though it was the hardest thing she'd ever had to do. But he wasn't about to give her up that easily.

He couldn't.

He might not be able to slide inside her but he had to do *something* to sate this storm that raged and howled inside him, demanding more of her. *Needing* more of her.

Dropping to his knees, he hooked the shred of lace to one side.

'Wait.' She struggled to sit up, breathless and flustered. 'What are you…?'

But he didn't give her time to finish, he wanted to taste her too badly. Sliding one of her legs over his shoulder, he lowered his head and licked his way straight into her. Her shaky cry, as her hands tangled into his hair, was all the validation he needed.

She tasted of slick, sweet honey, and Sol couldn't get enough. He played with her, toyed with her, drawing lazy whorls with his tongue all around her swollen, molten core, before sliding over her, sliding into her, sucking on her, making her hips meet his mouth with each thrust.

And then she was moving faster, her breathing more ragged than ever, and he gripped hold of her and held her fast, prolonging her agony and ecstasy.

'Sol…please…' she rasped out.

As if she was all his for the taking.

The thought lanced through him with more appeal than it had any right to do.

With one finger sliding inside her, he licked faster and sucked harder. Anouk cried out, bucked against him, and shattered on his tongue. Fragmenting all around him. But he wasn't finished. Over and over he pushed her past the edge until he knew she could fall no more and, reluctantly, he sat back.

He re-buttoned his shirt, locating his jacket and bow tie with surprisingly shaky hands. At least it gave him time to recover, lest he lose all sense of self and pull her onto him to sate them both, there and then.

He watched her as she finally began to come back to herself. God, but she was beautiful. The need to have her still pounded through him, leaving him edgy and restless in a way he'd never experienced before.

Her eyes flickered to him, seeming to focus. 'You're dressed?'

The distraught shadow in those blue pools caught at him, pulling into a tight band around his chest. Around his sex.

'I have to go back out to the gala,' he gritted out. 'It's my role to raise money. For the charity.'

'Of course.' She pulled her mouth into a semblance of a smile although he wondered what it cost her. 'This was sex. Just sex.'

And there was no reason for that to grate on him as it did.

'And tonight, I intend there to be much more of it,' he growled. 'Properly. When we can take our time.'

'More?' Her hand fluttered to her chest and he found he rather liked it.

'Much more,' he echoed firmly. 'Trust me, Anouk. That was just for starters.'

And then, before she could answer he spun around and left the room, not trusting himself.

He had a duty to the charity, and the kids. But if he stayed another moment with Anouk, he wasn't sure he could trust himself not to give in to temptation in the form of this bright, focussed, driven doctor with the blonde hair that sparkled like a glorious beach, and the blue eyes that made him sink fathoms deep.

And, goodness, he could still taste her sweetness on his tongue; still smell her on his fingers. And it was driving him to distraction.

She was driving him to distraction.

Who would have thought that the demure, strait-laced Anouk Hart would have ended up being his kryptonite?

CHAPTER FIVE

SOL SLAMMED HIS car door shut with a vicious whack of his arm and made his way across the hospital car park.

He'd been in a foul mood since the Gala.

Leaving Anouk in that room after such a teaser of her luscious body had been nearly impossible. Promising them both a night full of more carnal discoveries had been the only way he'd managed to get back out to the gala to carry out the role that had brought him there in the first place: to raise money and awareness for the young carers, the kids who already had enough responsibility for people in their lives, and he refused to let them down.

Even for Anouk.

But he couldn't have anticipated that things would become so chaotic with Malachi, who had had to leave. It hadn't occurred to him that the night with Anouk might not happen. But his body had been protesting it ever since.

Even this morning he'd woken in the early hours, his head full of images of Anouk, his body hard and ready. He would swear he could still taste her on his tongue; still close his eyes and feel the heat from her body against his chest. And decidedly lower.

As if he were an overeager adolescent.

When had any woman invaded his every thought like this? When had any woman made him...*pine* for her? It simply wasn't his usual style.

Yet worse than any of that had been the fact that he'd wanted to tell her that he wasn't as bad as his reputation painted him. Perhaps ten years ago he'd been a playboy, even eight years ago. But recently, between his career and the charity, he didn't have time to seduce the sheer volume of women the rumours would have Anouk believe.

But, to what end?

What would it change?

He might no longer have the time, or the same inclination, for one-night stands with an endless procession of pretty, eager partners—but that hardly meant he was suddenly going to turn into the kind of commitment-ready man that a woman like Anouk would demand.

She might still be haunting his brain, and his body, in a way that no other woman ever had, but that was surely just because that all too brief encounter in the office hadn't quite been enough to slake their desire for one another. He still couldn't offer her any more than no-strings sex.

So then why care whether his reputation was entirely accurate? It was close enough, wasn't it? What did it matter *what* Anouk Hart thought of him?

Disgusted with himself, he had thrown the bedsheets back and stomped down to his home gym, running, rowing and carrying out a brutal training routine designed to really push his body. As if it could drive out the gnawing hunger he felt inside.

He shouldn't want her with such hunger.

Attraction was one thing, but this desire he felt for Anouk was something infinitely more dangerous. It made him wonder, just for a moment, what a normal relationship would be like. And that was much too treacherous a path because he wasn't like most normal people. He didn't have that capacity for love that they had.

Hadn't his childhood taught him that? When his mother had been at her most vulnerable, when she'd most needed his care, he'd resented her. Hated her, even.

He had never gone to visit her in that centre Malachi had managed to get her into when he'd been fifteen. He'd only gone to her funeral a year later because Malachi had practically dragged him there by his ear. And he had resented every single second of it. Hadn't he given that woman enough of his precious time and attention? Hadn't he sacrificed his childhood for her? And hadn't Malachi sacrificed even more?

All of which meant he wasn't the kind of man for a woman like Anouk. He didn't love a person, flaws and all. No, he honed in on any imperfections and magnified them until he couldn't see past them to the person beneath. He used those flaws against them and Anouk deserved better than that.

She deserved better than him. If he thought anything of her at all then he would stay away from her.

At least the punishing training regime of the last couple of days seemed to have distracted his body. Hopefully, the demands of a shift in Neurology would occupy his head, as well.

What he hadn't expected was to be called straight down to Resus only to find he was once again needed on Anouk's team.

As if fate were personally throwing them together, he griped, striding through the doors only to come face to face with the woman who occupied too much of his brain. She stared at him in shock for several long seconds before dropping her eyes and switching back into professional mode.

Just like Anouk. Sol couldn't help grinning to himself. He would have been disappointed if she hadn't done so but at least she seemed as disquieted about his appearance as he felt. That was perhaps some consolation.

She cleared her throat and he knew he didn't imagine that overly bossy tone was meant for him.

'Okay, team, can you gather round a moment, please? We have a twenty-month-old girl who fell frontwards down a flight of concrete steps. ETA five minutes. Blood loss, but breathing and conscious. Helipad response team have gone up to the roof now to meet the HEMS. We're just waiting for now.'

The team moved quickly, getting equipment, a fresh mattress, the right materials—a flurry of activity as they prepared for the new patient to arrive. And when it all stilled, he wasn't prepared for Anouk to be standing right in front of him, a startled look on her face as though she hadn't expected to turn around and find him there.

He tried reminding himself of all the reasons he should keep his distance, but suddenly he couldn't think of a single one of them.

'I see I'm not the only one to have been brightening up this place.'

Sol jerked his head to the two-foot counter-top Christmas tree, prettily decorated, on the centre computer tables. He had no idea where they came from, yet the words tripped off his tongue, low and teasing.

'I didn't do it,' she retorted quickly.

Perhaps a little too quickly. And the way she flushed a deep scarlet made him unexpectedly curious. Was there something more to the story? Something that made her blush like a schoolgirl in front of him? Sol discovered he rather liked that idea.

'Ah, but do you know who did?' He took a stab in the dark, delighted when it seemed to pay off as her blush didn't fade, but she did manage to look simultaneously murderous.

As well as ridiculously cute.

'No.'

'Isn't that odd? I don't think I believe you,' he offered soberly, earning him a long-suffering eye-roll.

It delighted him beyond all measure.

'Fine. Saskia did it,' she bit out. 'Now will you leave it alone?'

'And you let her?' he heard himself asking. Laughing.

'I let her?' Anouk folded her arms across her chest.

'You let her decorate Resus? After the go you had at me for the bit of tinsel? Or did my words make you reconsider your rather military stance?'

Anouk scowled. He was obviously baiting her, so the last thing she should do was rise to it.

'You think a lot of yourself, don't you? And for the record, I don't control Saskia.'

'I never suggested you did.' He grinned, beginning to enjoy himself now. 'But she's your best friend. I dare say she wouldn't have done it if you'd asked her not to.'

She glowered, continuing to eye him silently, for several beats too long.

'Fine,' she conceded eventually, grudgingly. Rolling her eyes at him and sending a lick of heat straight through to his sex. 'I thought it might be nice.'

'Nice, huh?'

'For the patients,' she huffed. 'You really do need to stop being so arrogant. I didn't do it because *you* suggested it.'

'Heaven forbid.'

He didn't even attempt to conceal his chuckles.

'In fact, like I said, I didn't even do it at all.'

'No, of course not. It was your friend. And I'm guessing you didn't help her one bit.'

Her bristly demeanour gave her away, and Sol grinned broadly. It was nonsensical how much lighter and happier, Anouk made things—even when she was irritated with him she managed to flip some unseen switch to turn his day from aggravating to enjoyable.

Even when she was dealing with a casualty,

he found his eyes lingered a fraction longer on Anouk. Something about her seeming to shine that little bit brighter than everyone else around her.

She was fascinating.

Which made her so much worse than simply *hot*.

Anouk had taken up residence in his head and was apparently claiming squatter's rights. He couldn't seem to eject her and the harder he tried, the deeper she seemed to insinuate herself.

Which left only one solution. A solution that he would never in his right mind have expected himself to consider, and that he couldn't imagine any other woman in the world bringing him to.

The only way to stop himself from thinking about Anouk Hart was to convince her that they hadn't finished what she'd started the other night. That they both wanted more. Which shouldn't be too hard, given the sexual chemistry still crackling between them right now.

But he refused to lead her on. Just because he would be breaking his rule about second dates—not that it had been a proper first date, given that she hadn't even let him take her to that ball—it didn't mean he was offering her anything more. He wasn't putting a relationship on the table.

Who are you trying to convince? The question popped, unbidden, into his head. *Anouk or yourself?*

He shoved it away for the nonsense it was, but its echo lingered, nonetheless.

He needed more of Anouk. He *craved* her. But it was clear that whatever madness—he flattered himself to think it was their intense attraction—had overcome her the night of the gala, she wasn't going to let it get to her a second time. Not without a fight.

She'd pulled down the *strait-laced* shutters and set up the blockades of *disapproval*. But she didn't quite manage to pull off *forbidding* with the same aplomb as before. There was a flash of memory in her expression, a spike of hunger in her glance.

He had no doubt that Anouk craved him every bit as much as he craved her. But her mind was trying to shut off all that her lush, rather wanton body was telling it.

Which meant that he was going to have to seduce her. *Court her*, as old Mrs Bowman would have said.

Old-fashioned, and prim.

But dammit all if a perverse portion of him didn't relish the thought a little bit too much.

Did she really have to let Solomon Gunn affect her like this? Anouk thought shakily, her eyes locked on the doors at the end of Resus, waiting for the HEMS team to walk in.

She had veered from horror at her lustful display the night of the gala, to regret that they had only enjoyed one single, fiery, sensational act that night and she yearned for more. For the past two days it had been impossible to empty her head of the most vivid, thrilling, X-rated dreams that had kept her entire body smouldering.

No wonder she could barely bring herself to look him in the eye now, for fear that her every last wanton thought was etched right across her face for him to read.

Even now her body pricked with awareness, and she folded her arms over her chest as though she could dull the ache in her heavy nipples, as she relived the feel of his thumb skimming over them.

Mercifully, the doors chose that moment to swing open and the HEMS team hurried in.

'This is Rosie, twenty months old,' the HEMS doctor began handover. 'Normally fit and well. Approximately one hour ago she was in the park with her mum when she tumbled a metre and a half down a flight of concrete steps. She has a laceration above her right eye and has had altered GCS. GCS is eleven. Primary diagnosis is that she has had concussion and a period of observation will determine whether there are any inter-cranial injuries. She's had two hundred of paracetamol and one milligram ondansetron.'

'Pupils?' Anouk checked.

'She won't open her eyes.' The HEMS doctor shook his head gently.

'Right.' She nodded. 'Sol…'

There was little need to say anything. As the neurology specialist, he was already beginning his obs, his low, calm pitch already reassuring the little girl who was beginning to respond to his gentle instruction.

She nodded to her team to begin a fresh set of obs, as they were already preparing to do, and turned back to the HEMS doctor.

'Mum came with her?'

'This is Mum.' He turned to locate the young

girl's mother, who was looking ashen but keeping herself together well.

'Okay, Mum.' Anouk smiled reassuringly. 'We're just going to check Rosie over for now, perhaps give her some medication to make her more comfortable, and then we'll be taking her for a scan to see what's going on with her head and neck. You're absolutely fine to stay here with her, let her see you, talk to her.'

'My husband is on his way...?' The mum trailed off uncertainly.

'That's fine. If he goes to the desk someone will bring him straight through to Resus.

'Thank you.' She smiled weakly, her eyes darting straight back to her daughter and her smile becoming deliberately brighter, her voice more upbeat as she tried to reassure the baby girl looking so small on the dark blue mattress.

As soon as they had completed their initial assessment they could wrap her in a blanket, which would stop her from looking quite so tiny and helpless. But Anouk didn't need the neurosurgeon beside her to tell her that, given Rosie's age, her little bones were still quite soft and the concern was that there could be an internal bleed, which might cause pressure and push the child's brain down.

Her team worked quickly and methodically, focussed on their task, feeding the information back to Anouk as she mentally constructed a picture for herself of what was going on with Rosie before preparing to take her little patient to CT.

'You're happy for the mother to accompany the child?' Sol's voice suddenly rumbled, low and rich in her ear, spreading through her body like luxuriously sticky caramel.

Anouk told herself not to be so stupid.

'Yes, I asked her if she was happy to join us before, so they'll be getting her leaded up.'

'Good,' he confirmed simply.

And there was no reason for her body to goosebump at the way they apparently worked so harmoniously together. No reason at all.

She thanked the HEMS team and wrapped up handover before getting straight back to her little patient and preparing her for CT.

'Do you fancy some lunch?' Sol asked quietly a couple of hours later, making her turn her head so fast that her neck cracked painfully. She pretended that it hadn't. 'It's a surprisingly quiet day today. I think we might actually be able to give it a try eating a meal for once.'

'Lunch?'

'Yes, the thing normal people eat around mid-day.'

'As opposed to the packet of biscuits I usually just about get time to grab?' She tried laughing to conceal her shock.

If she hadn't known Sol better, it might have sounded like an actual date.

'Hence why I want to buy you lunch.'

The temptation to accept was shockingly strong.

'Why?' she demanded instead.

He didn't even blink.

'I thought that, perhaps after the other night, it might be nice to get to know each other a little better. That is to say, *with* our clothes on.'

'Shush,' Anouk hissed, spinning wildly around before bustling him into an empty side room. 'Someone might hear you.'

'They didn't. So, lunchtime?'

'Like…a date?' she demanded stiffly. 'I don't think that's a good idea.'

His mouth crooked upwards.

'Don't panic, it's just lunch. No date.'

'It isn't *just* anything. It's about the optics.'

'No one cares.'

She rolled her eyes at him.

'Lots of people care. And even if they didn't, *I* care.'

'That you're seen on a lunch date at work? Or that you're seen with me?'

'Both. And I thought you said it wouldn't be a date?'

His grin ramped up until it made her stomach tighten. And other things tighten, too.

'I lied.' He winked at her, making her tingle now, too.

She was pretty sure he knew exactly what he was doing. That he could read every embarrassing effect on her hot face.

'You're irredeemable,' she snapped.

'Thanks.'

'It wasn't a compliment.'

'Too late. I took it as one.' He rocked back and leant on the doorjamb, folding his arms over his chest in a way that he must surely know made him look all the more hewn and powerful. All male.

She cursed her faithless heart and the tattoo

it was currently beating throughout every vein and nerve-ending in her body. His dark eyes—as glossy and mesmerising as a master chocolatier's darkest mirror glaze—rippled with something she couldn't read but traitorously wished she could.

She ought to back up and put a little distance between the two of them. Or, better yet, leave. Instead, she stayed exactly where she was. Within arm's reach of Sol. A silent invitation even as she pretended it wasn't.

The lazy, insouciant way he watched her warned her that he knew it was pretence. His eyes raked over her body and left it as tingling and *aware* as she'd been that night. Craving more. She couldn't tear her gaze from that mouth, wicked and expert all at once. The things it had done to her should be illegal.

She was glad they weren't.

Everything inside was still. Calm. Expectant.

'Is something wrong?' he demanded suddenly.

And Anouk was aware of an edge to his tone. A hint that he was teasing her, playing with her, but she didn't know what the joke was.

'Wrong?'

'You appear to be rather fixated.'

'Fixated?'

She was beginning to sound a little like the old neighbour's parrot that had had a habit of waking her and Saskia at ridiculous hours in the morning, despite the fact that it was a decent apartment and the walls weren't exactly thin.

'With my mouth?'

She snapped her eyes up.

'I'm not fixated with your mouth.'

'Indeed? Only, I was going to ask if there was something there. A mark perhaps. An ink stain. A crumb.'

God help her, but all she could think of now was that if it had been a crumb, she would have gladly licked it off.

'No crumb,' she managed briskly. 'Or anything else.'

'Shame.'

As though he could read her illicit thoughts.

'I should go.'

'You should,' he agreed.

It took a great effort to galvanise her legs, moving one in front of the other in a great imitation of a newborn foal. Was it any wonder then that as she reached Sol and he refused to budge to let her pass easily, she faltered slightly?

He caught her in an instant, not that she had been about to fall, and suddenly she was being hauled into his arms, and he was holding her there, and she couldn't breathe. All she could do was stare again at his fascinating mouth, silently begging it to come crashing down on hers as it had that night.

When it didn't, Anouk didn't see any other choice but to lean up and press her lips to his.

It was instant combustion. His arms encircled her, pulling her to him. Her soft, pliant body against his deliciously hard one. He dipped his head and tasted her, sampling as though she were some precious vintage wine, leaving Anouk feeling revered and rare.

He dipped in and out, making her arch to him for more, soft moans escaping her lips in spite of herself.

He let his fingers tangle in her hair, mumbling words like *glorious* and *spun-silk gold*.

'It's just hair,' she muttered against his mouth, half afraid that she would fall for his charms when she knew better, probably better than anyone.

'No,' he argued, drawing back from her and tangling his hands deep within the abundance.

'It's like running my fingers through the softest gallium.'

'I don't need the hollow compliments...' she began, but when he raked his thumb over her lower lip, apparently revelling in the feel of her shaky breath on his skin, she found she couldn't even remember what she'd been about to say.

All the while she wanted the moment to last an eternity, maybe two, and yet also wanted the journey to be over, so that he could finally take her to his apartment and release the madness that had been building ever since he'd pressed his head between her legs that night and showed her exactly what she'd been missing all these years. With her two perfectly nice, perfectly dull boyfriends.

He kissed her some more. Slowly, reverently, as though they had all the time in the world and as though they weren't in the middle of a busy hospital.

The hospital, the voice sounded dully through the fog of her brain.

Her shift.

She had no idea from where she found the strength to break his kiss. And then some more, to break his hold.

'This is what you do, isn't it?' she managed in a strangled voice.

'Does it matter? If we're both enjoying it?'

She couldn't tell him that *yes, it mattered.* Especially when he made her feel as though she were special, only to remember that she wasn't.

That a hundred girls had probably travelled this same road before.

Idiot that she was.

'I have work to do,' she bit out, whirling around and snatching open the door before she could do something as stupid as change her mind.

The last thing she expected was to hear his voice carry, deep and smooth, down the hall.

'Come with me to the centre.'

She shouldn't let him worm his way under her skin. She *shouldn't.*

'Say that again?' she demanded, stopping and turning slowly.

'Come with me to see the Care to Play centre. See what it's all about.'

He was offering to show her into his private world? His private life? She could hardly believe he would be that open with her. Or anyone, for that matter.

By the expression that fleetingly clouded Sol's

face, he could hardly believe it either. If she didn't accept quickly, she feared he might rescind the invitation. And, despite all her promises to herself to steer clear of him after the gala, she desperately didn't want him to rescind anything.

Solomon Gunn.

He'd been worming his way under her skin ever since she'd met him. She'd staved him off initially by fixing on his playboy reputation. It hadn't been too difficult, not after watching her self-destructive mother make one poor choice after the next where bad boys were concerned.

Yet, she'd also seen flashes of another side of Sol. A compassionate side lacked by other top-flight surgeons she knew. The incident with young Izzy and her family, if she was going to be honest now, hadn't been the first. Nor the care for his old patient—Mrs Bowman.

But that didn't mean she had to be attracted to him, did it? She was supposed to be immune, for pity's sake.

Anouk was still giving herself a halfway decent talking-to when she heard her own voice replying.

'Okay.' No, not really *okay*, her brain screamed at her to take it back. 'I'd like to see the centre.'

'Then I'll bring you some forms to sign.'

'Forms?'

'Standard security. For being with the kids. As a doctor you'll be fine, but it protects the centre.'

'Right.'

By the book, Sol? Anouk said nothing but filed it away. It was yet another sign of how much this centre, and these kids, meant to him.

Reckless playboy? Or caring protector? Every time she thought she knew him, he morphed into something else. She couldn't pin him down.

It mattered to her more than it had any right to.

CHAPTER SIX

'WELL,' ANOUK MUTTERED to herself as she slapped her steering wheel lightly. 'You've been sitting out here for nearly half an hour. Here goes nothing.'

Yanking open her door, she jackknifed out of her car, clicked the lock button, and marched to the centre before she could talk herself out of anything.

She was barely through the doors before an older woman stopped her.

'Can I help you?'

'I'm Anouk,' she began. 'Anouk Hart. I…'

She trailed off. Should she say she was here to meet Sol? Or just that he'd given her forms to fill out the other day? Or perhaps she shouldn't mention him at all; she didn't want people to think she was just using the centre to somehow wheedle her way in with him.

'Oh, yes, Anouk.' The woman smiled. 'I'm

Barbara. Sol has been telling us all about you. So have Izzy and Katie.'

'The girls are here?'

'Yes, Katie particularly, of course. Izzy only got out of hospital yesterday but the first thing she did was ask when you would be coming in.' Barbara laughed.

'It always amazes me how resilient kids are.' Anouk shook her head. 'Only a week ago she was in my Resus department.'

'Now she's home and already back to helping her mum,' the woman agreed. 'Inspirational. Just like so many of the kids I see come through those doors.'

'I can see why Sol cares so much about this place. I guess not everyone with a privileged childhood wants to see what other people have to go through.'

'I know. I like to think that's why Sol—and Malachi, for that matter—set up this place. They might be rich, influential men now, but neither of them has ever forgotten how appalling their own childhoods were.'

Anouk blinked. She fought to keep her expression neutral.

'Right.'

'I mean, not just as young carers themselves but how they had to drag themselves out of the gutter,' Barbara continued, clearly under the impression that this wasn't news to Anouk. 'Without them getting the message out, people with clout wouldn't even know about us. This centre, and the new one they are building, simply wouldn't exist.'

Anouk made a sound of acknowledgement, but her head was spinning.

Sol had been a young carer? He had dragged himself out of the gutter?

It didn't make any sense. But what confused her most was that Barbara didn't seem worried about discussing it. As though it was common knowledge.

As though she was talking about a completely different Solomon Gunn from the playboy neurosurgeon who relished his Smoking Gun nickname.

Was it possible that his colleagues didn't know the man at all?

Even she herself sometimes forgot how other people envied her childhood when they knew she was the daughter of a late Hollywood actress. They couldn't see the darker, uglier side of that life. Was it the same for Sol? People said he was a wealthy neurosurgeon, coming from money, and they made judgements. *She* had made judgements.

Would the real Solomon Gunn please step forward?

'So, anyway, we thought you might like to spend the afternoon with Libby. She's a friendly little girl, six, sole carer for her mother, although...' Barbara paused, half stating, half questioning '...you'll know that we don't discuss that side of things here?'

'Yes, I know. This is a place she can come and just be a child.'

The woman nodded her approval.

'At the moment Libby is making Father Christmas faces for the Christmas Fayre. Are you any good at crafting?'

'I'm not known for it.' Her laugh betrayed a hint of nerves, but that couldn't be helped. 'But I'm keen to learn. Sol isn't here?'

'There was a problem at the construction site. Besides, I think he thought you might find it easier getting to know the children in your own time.'

Without him looking over her shoulder, did he mean? Either way, it was odd but, taking the complication of having to interact with Sol out of the equation, she could practically *feel* some of her tension slipping from her shoulders, through her body to the floor, and away from her.

She exhaled quietly with relief.

'That probably would be better.'

Was it her imagination, or did Barbara's smile suddenly seem brighter? Wider?

'That will do just fine,' Barbara approved, leading her over to where a young girl sat, with a unicorn T-shirt and pink jeans, her hair plaited exceptionally neatly either side of her head.

'Libby, I've got another set of helping hands. This is Anouk. You remember Izzy and Katie mentioned her.'

A six-year-old girl glanced up with a wide, toothy smile.

'And Sol talked about her, too,' she added. 'You're just in time to help me decorate the next lot of faces to stick on the goodie bags. Can you bring those cotton-wool balls over there for the beard? I've got the googly eyes but we'll cut little red hats out of the felt and use a mini pompom for the bobble.'

Before she knew it, Barbara had gone, leaving Libby and Anouk alone. Not that it seemed to matter since Libby was quite happy to take charge.

'What if you cut the felt hats and I'll stick them on?' Libby suggested. 'Wait, no, not like that. Like this. Let me show you.'

Quickly, efficiently, Libby demonstrated what she wanted, talking Anouk through each step, not that it seemed particularly complicated. Yet the way the girl approached the crafting task with such meticulousness and attention to detail, in a way that was common in six-year-olds, reminded her of Libby's experience as a young carer.

Her chest kicked. It was an unexpected reminder of her own childhood, when she had organised her mother with care and discipline as though she were Annalise Hartwood's personal assistant rather than her daughter.

And verbal punching bag, of course.

Her brain skittered away from the unwanted memories.

'Are you looking forward to Christmas?' Anouk

asked milliseconds before it occurred to her that it might not be the most appropriate question for someone like Libby.

For a moment, the little girl looked thoughtful and then, to Anouk's relief, she managed a slow bob of her head. Anouk hadn't realised she'd been holding her breath until that moment.

'Yes, I think so. It's a lot better now that I have this place to come to.'

'Right,' Anouk agreed, swallowing quickly. 'And these are for the Christmas Fayre?'

'Yep, it's a lot of fun. There are stalls and fairground games, and Sol and Malachi usually arrange something special. Like, one year it was an ice rink, and another it was fairground rides. It can be a chance for the centre to get out into the community and show them that we're good kids.'

'I understand.' Anouk bobbed her head, carefully concealing her surprise.

The maturity with which Libby spoke belied her six years. But then, that was likely a result of being a child carer for her parent. It was testament to her resilience how this little girl could talk so eloquently one moment, and be excited about making Father Christmas faces to stick on paper bags of stocking fillers.

'Plus, we raise money to help keep the centre running,' she added proudly. 'And to buy new pieces for our Christmas village scene.'

Anouk wasn't quite sure what that was, but before she could ask Libby was reaching for a small box beside her to lift up a handful of faces from Santa to Rudolph, and from elves to gingerbread men.

'I made these already.'

'They're amazing.'

Libby beamed, dropping her voice to a conspiratorial whisper.

'And, don't tell the younger girls, but I know that Father Christmas isn't real.'

'What makes you think that?' Anouk asked carefully. Most six-year-olds she knew still believed.

Libby shot her a cynical smile.

'Please. I know he isn't. Last year, when I was five, we went shopping together and Mummy bought me presents without me knowing. But over Christmas she got unwell again and couldn't get out of bed without my help so she couldn't put them out overnight. She tried to pretend that Father Christmas had got lost and left them under her bed by mistake.'

'That's entirely possible,' Anouk replied steadily, her eyes deliberately focussed on her task.

'You don't have to protect me. I'm not your average six-year-old,' Libby remonstrated softly, echoing words she must have heard people use time and again about her.

The matter-of-fact tone only tugged at Anouk's heart all the harder.

'The point is that Mummy was ill so I'd had to do the hoovering over Christmas. I knew the presents had been there for weeks. I tried to tell Mummy but she got upset and cross with herself so I pretended that I believed her.'

'It's still possible—'

Libby cut her off as though she hadn't spoken.

'But I wanted to tell someone and I like you. I think I can trust you.' She tipped her head on one side and eyed Anouk shrewdly. 'I can, can't I?'

The lump in her throat meant she might as well have been trying to swallow a golf ball.

'You can,' she choked out, and Libby just eyed her a little longer before bending her head back to her Father Christmas crafting and working diligently again. A companionable silence settled over them once more—as long as the little girl couldn't hear how hard and how fast Anouk's heart was beating for her, that was.

A good half-hour had to have passed before Libby spoke again.

'You know there's going to be an entertainer at the Christmas Fayre, maybe a magician or a puppet show?'

As if their previous conversation had never happened.

'Wow.' Anouk hoped she managed to inject just the right amount of sounding impressed but not condescending. 'That sounds like it will be fun.'

'It will.' The girl nodded enthusiastically. 'Especially when it's a real entertainer and not just Sol and Malachi dressed up in costumes. Although they're pretty funny, too. And so cool.'

'You think so?' She tried to sound chatty but her throat felt dry. Scratchy.

Libby's unbridled adoration didn't help Anouk in her fight not to let Sol get under her skin any more than he had already appeared to.

'Of course—' Libby snorted in a little-girl sort

of way '—you could normally see it for yourself. They're usually always here. Or at least, they used to be before they started to build our new centre.'

Picking up another face to glue, Anouk tried to sound utterly casual.

'What makes them so cool, then?'

'Well, *everything*, I guess.' Libby looked up, her expression thoughtful. 'They were carers, too, just like all of us, only my mummy loves me and their mummy didn't. But they've still become rich and famous. When I grow up, I'm going to be just like them.'

'A surgeon like Sol?'

It was all she could do to sound normal. Another revelation about Sol. Another description that made him seem like a world away from the commitment-phobic playboy of the hospital gossip mill.

'Sol's a *neurosurgeon*,' Libby corrected. 'He saves lives. Or maybe I'll be an investor and become a millionaire like Malachi. I haven't decided yet, but they're both always saying that if you want something enough, and work hard enough for it, there's a good chance that you can achieve it.'

'Right.' Anouk grappled for something to say.

She wasn't sure if it was Libby's maturity or the fact that Sol was such an inspiration to the little girl that stole her breath away the most.

'Did you know they like to help to actually build the new centre?'

'Sorry?' Anouk snapped back to the present.

'Sol and Malachi?' Libby prompted. 'They are actually helping to build the new Care to Play. We saw them a lot in the summer when the centre organised rounders and football matches in the park. They were carrying bags off a builder's truck and cutting wood.'

'They did?' The image certainly didn't do anything to dampen the ache that constantly rolled inside her these days.

No wonder Sol always looked so healthy. Every time she had failed to push away memories of that mouth-watering physique, slick and hot under her hands, she'd consoled herself with the knowledge that he must spend countless hours in the gym. Her mother had enjoyed enough gym-junkie boyfriends for her to know that they loved themselves more than they would ever be able to love someone else.

She'd almost convinced herself that this fact

therefore detracted from how good-looking Sol might otherwise seem. So discovering now that he had achieved that honed, utterly masculine body from genuine physical labour—and not just any labour, but building a centre for young carers—only made it that much harder to pretend there wasn't some empyreal fire to the man.

'Some of the older girls said they were hot.' Libby looked sceptical, all of her six years suddenly showing. 'But I think they were probably okay because they'd taken their tops off to cool down. They put them back on when we passed, though.'

'Right,' Anouk managed. Just about.

She imagined that the temperature of the brothers wasn't the kind of *hot* the older girls had meant. But the image of Sol shirtless wasn't one she was ready to deal with right at this moment.

'Sometimes we take them bottles of water to help cool them down.'

Despite herself, Anouk suppressed a grin.

'Very thoughtful of you.'

Libby, her eyes on her Santa face, didn't notice.

'Sol and Malachi look after us, it's only fair

that we do a little for them. They're who we buy the Christmas village scenes for. It's special to them.'

'I'm pretty sure they're looking after you because you already take care of people,' Anouk said softly.

'Well…maybe, but they know exactly what we're going through, and that makes it easier to talk about.'

Another titbit of information. Anouk felt like a tiny bird, starving for every morsel dropped about Sol. She bit her lip.

'How did they come to be carers?'

She'd tried to sound casual, but the little girl glanced up sharply.

'That's their story to tell.' Libby shut down immediately, sounding for all the world like a young woman and not a six-year-old kid. 'Don't you think?'

It was all Anouk could do not to let it show how flustered she felt. She plastered a smile on her face. She wouldn't think about Sol Gunn a second longer.

'Okay, Libby, I've finished that batch of Father Christmas faces. What should I make now?'

And she wouldn't be going anywhere near the new building site, either.

Sol knew she was there even before he turned around. It was as though the entire air seemed to change and shift around him and where it had been peaceful before, now a kind of energy was pulsating through it.

He took a breath and took his time, turning slowly. She looked delicious standing there, all bundled up in a big coat, a Christmas pudding hat and a very green, Christmas-tree-patterned scarf.

'Anouk.' Even her name tasted absurdly good as it rolled off his tongue. 'Just passing?'

'Don't be fatuous,' she replied evenly. 'Libby said I could find you here. As I imagine you knew she would.'

He wanted to deny it but couldn't.

Libby was confident and talkative, a good kid who would have been able to show Anouk around without becoming tongue-tied. But he supposed there was a tiny piece of him that had also known the six-year-old would have told Anouk about the new centre.

He just hadn't known, until now, whether

Anouk would have taken the bait and come to see him for herself. He tried to ignore the sense of satisfaction that punctured him.

'Ah, but you didn't have to come.'

'Of course that's what your response would be.' She drew her lips into a thin line.

Yet Sol couldn't help but notice that it wasn't a denial either. He was barely even aware of dropping his tools and making his way to her, feeling the heat start to come back to his frozen limbs as he stamped his way over the stony ground.

'So why *are* you here?'

'Libby mentioned that you and Malachi are helping to build the place. I had to come and see for myself, and here you are, hauling bags of...' she cocked her head to read the packaging that he still had hoisted on his shoulder '...plaster off a truck. Surely you have guys to do that for you?'

'Every bit Mal and I do means more money saved for the centre itself.'

Plus, the physical labour of it somehow... fulfilled him.

'I thought you were a millionaire playboy? You and your brother come from money. Isn't that what the hospital grapevine says?'

He opened his mouth to make one of his typical, non-committal responses, but found he couldn't. There was a new edge in her tone, almost as if she was testing him. But she couldn't possibly know the truth, could she?

Something dark and unfamiliar loomed in the shadows of his mind. A lesser man might have mistaken it for shame at his past. But he refused to be that lesser man. Malachi was right: it was done. It was history. No need to rake up the humiliation of their childhood for anyone, especially the daughter of a Hollywood starlet who had no doubt enjoyed a charmed upbringing.

Except that wasn't what the Hintons had said, was it?

He stuffed it down and forced himself to be upbeat.

'Mal and I can donate all we want, but these centres need to exist for themselves, support themselves—that way they can keep going long after we're gone. And if the model works then it can be replicated up and down the country.'

'You want more Care to Play centres,' she realised.

'Right. One centre is good, two centres is even

better, but what we want is a business model which can be extended nationally.'

'I…didn't think of that.'

'Why would you?' he asked. 'Want a tour?'

Anouk looked surprised, before bouncing her Christmas pudding hat slowly and looking even more ridiculously cute.

'Sure. Why not?'

'So, what happened with that toddler who fell down the concrete steps?' he asked as he turned and headed into the building as if it made no difference to him whether she had followed or not. It was only as he lowered the plaster bag and heard her boots clicking on the concrete floor that he knew she had.

Why did it give him another jolt of victory?

How had this woman managed to insinuate her way under his skin? It was sheer insanity and he should walk away now.

Sol had the oddest sensation that if he didn't walk now, it would be too late.

And still he unlocked the padlock and unwound the heavy-link chain from around the temporary plywood doors.

'The twenty-month-old?' Anouk looked surprised.

'Yeah. Rosie, right?'

'Yes, Rosie. Believe it or not she was okay.' Anouk grinned, the miraculous recovery of kids never failing to amaze her. 'You knew there were no obvious signs of any breaks or fractures?'

'I did, but there was that inter-cranial bleed that needed to be monitored.'

'Yep, that's it. She stayed in for two nights before being cleared. She was discharged yesterday.'

'Lucky.' He smiled.

'Very.'

'Anyway, welcome to our new Care to Play centre.' He slid the chain through one door handle and pulled the other open to usher her inside. 'We should be in by the new year.'

Anouk walked through what would soon be the reception area, stopping dead practically in the doorway of the new hall. Then she glanced around, silently taking it all in. From the expansive, hi-tech-looking space with its spaghetti junction of wires, evidently in preparation for any number of new gadgets for the kids, and the large heaters to dry the plaster.

It was inexplicable how buoyed up he felt, showing her around and watching her reaction—

this unique, complicated woman who pulled at something deep inside him—and he didn't know what name to put to it.

He didn't really want to try.

There was an attraction, certainly, but he'd been attracted to plenty of women in his time. A primal, sexual attraction.

This wasn't that.

He grappled for the word but the only thing he could come up with was...*connection*. And he knew better than to believe that.

Didn't he?

'What's going over there?' she asked, pointing to an area of the room where there was still a fair amount of work to do.

'A stage.' Sol smiled. 'You want to see the talent some of these kids have. They're just bursting for a forum in which they can showcase what they can do. Behind the wall there are a couple of soundproofed music rooms, too. We'll be putting instruments in them and the kids can set up their own bands if they want to. Or just sing, whatever they want.'

'Goodness, this place really is so much bigger than where they are now.'

'By a couple of hundred square metres,' Sol

agreed. 'But it isn't just that, it's the way we've teched the place up.'

'I get that.' She smiled, with the kind of radiance that heated up a person's very bones. Heated up *his* very bones, anyway. 'It's incredible. The kids are going to be bowled over.'

'That's the hope. Come on, I'll show you the rest.'

He continued the tour to the new kitchens, the offices, the music rooms, and finally the small quiet rooms.

'Although the centre is built on the idea that kids can come in and talk about normal things, and just be a kid crafting, or playing, or singing, there are nonetheless times when kids *will* need to talk. Maybe a little group of them will get together.'

'And support each other,' Anouk offered.

'Exactly. Or sometimes someone might just need a quiet room for a one-on-one chat with an adult. We do get kids who have been self-harming and need something more to help them cope. They might have been struggling without any support and things have just got on top of them and they haven't known where to turn.'

He didn't miss the way Anouk dropped her

eyes from his, that familiar stain creeping over her skin whenever she was embarrassed.

'Everything okay?'

'So Care to Play can be there for them and make sure they know that they're no longer alone?' she trotted out stiffly. 'That's great.'

Spinning around, she lunged for the door to leave and practically bumped into him.

Instinct made him reach out and grab her upper arms to steady her, before he could stop himself. There was clearly something more going on here and he felt oddly driven to find out what it was.

But the instant he made physical contact with her, electricity charged through him, practically fusing his hands in place. He was wholly unable to pull away. The need to learn more about this woman who had infiltrated his whole being in a matter of a week was almost visceral.

'What's going on, Anouk?' Urgency laced through his voice. 'What is it?'

These rooms were designed to feel closed off. A place where kids could talk about the things they might not even want to admit to themselves. *Safe*.

Right now, with Anouk up against his chest

and his nostrils suddenly full of that fresh, faintly floral scent that he associated with her alone, Sol felt about as far from safe as it was possible to get.

He glanced down to see the pulse in her slender neck jolt then quicken, which didn't exactly help matters. The need to bend his head to hers and taste her lips again was almost overpowering.

Almost.

It was only the need to wait for her answer, to understand her better, that held him back. It made no sense and yet he ached to hear her talk to him as though he was someone other than a morally bankrupt tomcat willing to jump on anything in a skirt.

And yet, if she did, was he ready to answer her?

CHAPTER SEVEN

SHE GLANCED UP at him, though he got the impression that it cost her dearly to do so. She watched him for what seemed like an eternity and, for a moment, he believed she was actually going to talk. To tell him…something that counted.

And then the shutters slammed down with a clang.

'I don't know what you're talking about.' She forced a smile, trying to inch discreetly back a fraction. Not that there was anywhere to go in this tiny space.

'I don't believe that.'

She glowered at him, but he didn't miss the way she swallowed. Hard.

He could push her. He wanted to. But something told Sol that would be counterproductive.

The moments ticked by.

'Why would I?' she demanded suddenly.

'Why would you what?'

'Why would I talk to you? Open up to you?' Her voice sounded angry and pained, and raw all at once. It spoke to him in a way he recognised only too well. 'When you wouldn't dream of talking to me.'

'I have talked to you,' he lied. 'I've invited you here. You've spent time with the kids only today.'

He made himself step back, pretending that her soft, plump lips weren't still imprinted in his mind's eye. And that the feel of her arms didn't still sear through his palms. He reminded himself that it was purely physical, sexual attraction, even if it felt alien.

Because what else *could* it be?

'You've told me lots about the kids, and the centre. Between the gala, and my visit, you've given me plenty of information. You've explained how there are lots of charities out there for young carers, and lots of volunteers, really good people, and how your charity is different. You've shown how it still isn't enough. These kids need more.'

'They do.'

'I agree.' She lifted her eyes to his, her gaze almost too intense to bear. 'My point is, Sol, that, in all the talking you've done, the one sub-ject you steer clear of is why you care so much.'

He hadn't seen it coming, but he should have. He should have been ready for the question. In a way, he was. And yet it still had the power to wind him.

His hands dropped from her arms and he swung away—the moment lost.

'Does it matter?' he managed, amazed at how calm, how cool, he sounded when inside his heart was pumping blood around his body as though he was a gold medal winning sprinter.

Behind him, she seemed to ponder for a mo-ment. Though whether about how to phrase her questions, or how she had come to ask them in the first instance, Sol couldn't quite be certain.

'I don't know,' she admitted. 'I suppose that's what I'm asking. If it matters.'

'I don't think I follow.'

'No,' she conceded, pulling her lips together as if she wasn't even sure what she was saying. 'It's just that *this* you isn't the image you tend to put forward of yourself. Solomon Gunn the playboy is well known, but it doesn't fit with all of...*this*.'

She waved her hand around the construction site that was the centre.

'I suppose I want to know which version of the man is really you. And if it's this one, then wouldn't you rather be Solomon Gunn, tireless advocate for young carers?'

'No.'

She blinked.

'Why not?'

Because it invited too many questions, too much scrutiny, his own childhood would inevitably come out and that wasn't a side of his life he wanted people to see when they looked at him.

As it was threatening to do now.

It was odd the way he wanted her to know he was more than just that playboy—as inexplicable as that was—but when it came to telling her, showing her, the truth, he found he couldn't contend with that either.

Because the truth made him feel ashamed. Lacking. It was a chunk of his life he would readily burn down, if only he could.

'Because I like my playboy lifestyle,' he lied with an aplomb that had been perfected over more than a decade.

And, possibly for the first time, he hated himself for it.

'Do you really?' she asked softly. 'Only, I'm beginning to wonder, from all the things I've been hearing about you today, how you have much time at all for quite the number of amorous conquests your reputation suggests.'

'I'm a skilled multitasker.' He feigned a laugh.

Anyone else would have bought into it. Anouk stared at him, unfazed.

'You'd have to be in two places at once. No one is that good at multitasking.'

It was as though she could see down to his soul.

He reminded himself that even if she did know some scraps of truth about him, that was all she knew. Scraps. Not the whole picture, and it would stay that way. However much he might loathe what he was about to do.

'Trust me, Anouk, you're not the first woman I've slept with who has mistaken sexual intimacy for a more profound connection, and thought it meant they *understood* me. But it's just sex, nothing more.'

She blanched, making him feel the cad he knew he was.

Better that than this irrational ache he had to buy into her better opinion of him.

As the silence tightened around him, seemingly weighed down with anticipation, the last thing he expected was for Anouk to rally.

'I suspect you care about these kids because you understand them better than you'd have your moneyed gala guests believe.'

'Not really,' he denied.

'Of course you do.' She held his gaze, refusing to cow to him. 'Because you were a young carer, too, Sol.'

Of all the things he'd expected Anouk might say, that certainly wasn't one of them. For one brief, heart-stopping moment, he wondered if he could bluff her.

He had the oddest sensation that he wouldn't be able to. She would see right through his façade. The realisation needled him.

Or was he more galled at the idea that some traitorous element of himself wanted her to see through it?

He had no idea how he kept his tone neutral.

'You've been talking to Barbara.'

She shook her head but he didn't believe her and determined to make no bones about it.

'I've warned her about sharing personal information before,' he growled. 'No matter who it's about, or who to.'

'It wasn't Barbara.' Anouk raised her eyebrows.

'Of course it was. It had to be.'

'Actually, Libby told me,' Anouk bit out finally. 'She also told me that you and your brother were young carers. For your mother.'

He couldn't answer. Couldn't even speak.

'What else did she say?' he gritted out when he felt as if he'd finally managed to work his tongue loose.

'That it was your story to tell, not hers,' Anouk admitted.

His short, sharp laugh—if that was what it could be called—bounced off the freshly plastered walls.

'That sounds like Libby.'

There was another beat of silence, which Anouk only broke after it had become more than awkward.

'So, it's true?'

He didn't answer. If he denied it he would feel as though he was betraying a six-year-old girl. At the same time, he had no idea what else to say.

'How young?' Anouk added at last.

He'd answered this question a thousand times to different kids over the years, or considered it not to be the business of any of his hospital colleagues. But somehow it was different with Anouk. He couldn't bring himself to send her home, yet he had no intention of sharing something so personal with her.

Even if a component of him wanted to.

All of a sudden he had to get out of there. This conversation—or perhaps the last few—with Anouk had left him feeling battered and bruised, as though he couldn't work out what he wanted from her.

It was an unfamiliar, unwelcome sensation. *Mostly.*

He should leave, but he found that he wanted to spend more time with her and therein lay the issue. The more Sol thought about it, the more he came to the conclusion that he only wanted her because he hadn't had her yet.

As distasteful as it was, there was no other explanation. No other reason why she should have him tied up in such knots.

The solution was to remedy that situation. To convince Anouk that it was in both their interests to finish what they'd started the night of the gala. Once they had indulged their mutual desire, the sweeping need would at last abate.

Surely it was inevitable?

'There's no electricity in this place yet,' he stated abruptly. 'Except for the temporary generator powering the heaters. But there's a decent coffee house on the high street.'

She stood still as they watched each other for a beat too long. He waited for her to make her excuses and leave, and he told himself that he didn't care either way.

And then, abruptly, she grabbed her bag and threw it onto her shoulder.

'Let's go, then.'

'I swear I've heard this Christmas song in the shops since November,' Anouk muttered as they opened the doors to the coffee house only to be blasted by the heat, the gorgeous smells, and the music.

She wasn't even sure what she was doing here. Only that her chest was tight with some nonsensical notion that Solomon Gunn might actually... open up to her. As much as she knew it was ridiculous, she couldn't eject it from her head.

'Or October.' Sol laughed, his earlier unease having apparently melted away as soon as they'd left the centre and she'd dropped her questions. 'Okay, you get the table, I'll get the drinks. Just tell me what you want.'

Anouk tried not to feel deflated. It shouldn't matter that he didn't want to trust her. She shouldn't let it bother her. Just as she hadn't let that moment back in the new centre get to her. When he'd held her so close that she'd been convinced he was going to kiss her again.

When she'd *ached* for him to kiss her again.

But he hadn't. He'd just dropped her as though the moment hadn't crept under his skin even a fraction of the way it had slunk under hers.

And then she'd badgered him about his life, his childhood, being a young carer. As if that could reveal a side of him that she could understand, relate to, trust. But to what end? It wasn't as if she wanted a relationship with him. She wasn't naïve enough to think any woman could tame a perennial playboy, and yet…there was something about him that simply didn't seem to fit with the reputation.

Or perhaps that was what she was telling herself to justify her incongruously wanton forwardness the night of the gala. The night she *still* couldn't bring herself to regret. Even though she knew she ought to.

Maybe wanting to trust him was more about herself than Sol. Perhaps it was her wanting to vindicate that uncharacteristic one-night stand—if you could even call it that—to explain her sudden foray into seductress territory.

And still, it ate away at her that the Sol whom the kids at the centre loved so much was so very different from the bad boy the hospital knew.

She coveted knowing that man, too.

Yet she couldn't push him. The harder she tried, the more she could see the shutters coming down and still she couldn't seem to make herself walk away.

'I'm going for the Christmas cinnamon roast coffee,' he concluded after perusing the board for a moment. 'What would you like?'

'Tea. Nothing fancy, just a plain one, please.'

He raised his eyebrows at her.

'This can't be a manifestation of your aversion to Christmas?'

'It isn't an aversion,' she denied awkwardly.

'You really hate this time of year that much?'

He was turning the tables so casually that she

couldn't be sure if it was deliberate or if he really couldn't help it. Nevertheless, she opened her mouth to tell him that *of course she didn't.*

'Pretty much.' She shrugged, the words popping out of their own volition. 'I know you don't feel the same. With your home-baked mince pies, and your gorgeous tree, and the Christmas village scene.'

Instantly his face changed and she sucked in a breath, not sure what she'd said.

'What about the Christmas village scene?'

His tone was too careful.

'I'm not sure,' she admitted cautiously. 'I don't actually know what Libby meant, she just told me that the kids from the centre do all they can to get together enough money to buy you and Malachi a new piece every year.'

She waited for him to push her on the subject, but instead his expression cleared and he dipped his head before striding to the counter, leaving her to find an available table. And remind herself to stop reading too much into everything that concerned Solomon Gunn.

'What are we doing here, Sol?' Curiosity made her drop the question even before he'd finished sliding the tray onto their table. 'I can't imagine you bring *dates* here. At least, not *after* you've already stripped them bare on the desk in an opulent study. Though perhaps before, when you're still trying to seduce them.'

He didn't answer straight away, sliding his coat off and dropping into the seat opposite her to stir his drink thoughtfully.

'I find myself as mystified as you are by this continuing...draw,' he answered enigmatically, sending her mind into a whirl analysing what he might mean by it.

So much for not reading too much into everything he said or did, she snorted quietly to herself.

'Which means what, exactly?'

'I'm debating that,' he told her. 'And I'm rapidly coming to the conclusion that these drawn-out, skirting-the-issue games don't appear to be getting us anywhere.'

'I'm not playing games.' Her indignation wasn't as sharp as she might have expected it to be.

'Therefore, I would like to propose something else,' he continued, as though she hadn't spoken. 'I contend that allowing it to play out seems to be the most logical conclusion.'

She couldn't quite dislodge the pocket of air blocking her throat.

'Play out?' she asked faintly. 'As in…?'

His smile was lethal enough to make her fear for her sanity.

'Sex.'

The statement sliced through the air between them, its simplicity robbing her of all thought for a moment; sending delicious shivers all the way down her spine.

'One night of pure, unrestrained pleasure,' he repeated, as though she might not have understood his meaning the first time—but for the wicked smile carved into his handsome face. 'A conclusion of that night at the gala.'

It was useless to pretend that a restlessness didn't roll right through her at the audacity of the man. Along with the rudest images of the hot, devilish expression on his face moments before he'd dipped his head between her legs and greedily drunk her in.

It was why, although every grey cell in her head was screaming at her to decline, she could only sit there, her body tense and…*needy*, as she stared at him in silence.

'But if we do, Anouk. Then there will have to be ground rules.'

'Ground rules?' she echoed faintly.

'To avoid confusion at a later date.'

'Avoiding confusion is good,' she conceded, her voice sounding thick and slow.

She felt as though she were outside her own body.

She ought to be telling him *no*. Instead, she just wanted to get the so-called ground rules agreed so they could get onto the meatier portion of the conversation.

Who was this strange woman inhabiting her body? And what had Sol done to the real her that night? She should be disgusted with herself; at how easily she seemed to be falling in with what Sol was suggesting.

Her weak acquiescence was all too reminiscent of her desperate mother.

And yet something niggled at Anouk, even if she couldn't quite place her finger on it.

Something in the way Sol sat, slightly more upright than usual. Or the way he appeared to be choosing his words deliberately. Or the intent look in his eyes. It all gave the impression that he wasn't nearly as blasé about it as he wanted her to believe.

Or possibly it was just in her imagination.

Either way, Anouk made the decision there and then to accept it at face value. When would she ever get the chance to act so daringly with someone who thrilled her the way that Sol did?

'Let me guess, the ground rules are that it's just sex?' she managed hoarsely. 'That it's just for the one night? That there are no troublesome, wild emotions complicating things afterwards?'

'Yes, to all three,' he growled. 'Except for the wild part.'

'Oh?' she managed.

'I intend it to get very wild,' he promised, his voice low and practically pulsing through her. 'And very hot. And very lustful.'

She thought she might have swallowed her tongue for a moment.

'I'd be disappointed if it was anything less,' she managed, at last.

She didn't quite recall moving, but suddenly they were both standing and Sol was helping her into her coat before enveloping her hand in his and leading her outside. They didn't stop, or debate it any longer, but he pulled Anouk close to him and began threading his way through the streets spilling over with Christmas shoppers.

Streets that were still slick and wet from the rain that had fallen whilst they'd been inside but that had now stopped. As if just for them. The darkness enclosed them, the coldness not able to bite into her.

She didn't know when it occurred to her that something wasn't right. Possibly around the same time that Sol slowed down, scanning all around them with a grim expression on his face.

'Something is going on,' he ruminated. 'The roads are too busy, even for this time of year.'

'And the traffic is going the wrong way,' Anouk concurred, twisting around to look. 'A road traffic accident, maybe? A main road closed? Diversions?'

It was one of the side-effects of being an A & E doctor: she could perceive a potential major accident like a sixth sense. Things just didn't... sit right.

'More than one road, I'd say, given the volume of traffic.'

'So a multiple-car RTA?'

'Something.' He nodded, sliding his phone out of his back pocket as they exchanged a glance.

'I don't have to make the call. If they need me, they'll call.'

'It's work,' she raised her eyebrows. 'We both know you're itching to make that call. Anyway, call it a sign.'

'I don't believe in signs,' he scoffed. 'You and I getting together is inevitable, Anouk. We both know it. We can't out run it, and however hard we try it will catch up with us. That need will wrap itself around us and topple us to the ground.'

'Then I'll just have to run faster.'

He laughed. An oddly sensuous sound.

'The faster you run, the further you get, the harder the fall will ultimately be.'

He hadn't even begun to make the call when it rang.

'Here goes.' Raising his eyebrows, Sol took the call.

When he let go of her hand, it felt too much like a loss. All Anouk could do was try to glean all she could from his terse responses. When he started moving, she hurried to keep up.

'It's a major incident,' he bit out, snapping his phone shut a few moments later. 'Some kind of gas explosion on Beechmoor Street. Multiple casualties; they're splitting them between us and the Royal.'

Saskia.

'That's around the corner from where I live,' Anouk cried. 'I have to get back there.'

He stopped momentarily, swinging back to her.

'It isn't safe. The area has apparently been evacuated.'

'I have to get home.' She stepped onto the kerb with the intention of hailing a taxi.

'You won't get a taxi,' Sol told her. 'They said it's gridlock towards the hospital. If we head around the north side on foot, we should make it to the hospital.'

Should she go? For a moment, Anouk wondered whether following Sol was sensible or not. But if people were injured...?

'Okay.' She dipped her head, hurrying after him as he raced ahead.

She hadn't been called, but if things were that serious then extra hands could only be welcome.

And then, her phone began ringing, too.

CHAPTER EIGHT

'BLOOD GAS IS BACK,' Anouk announced to her team. 'She's got a pH of seven point zero four with a lactate of nine.'

'Bicarb?' her colleague asked.

She checked the screen.

'Eight. Basics are minus twenty. Okay, guys, let's go back to the beginning. Airway?'

She waited for her team to communicate that it was unobstructed before moving on.

'Breathing?'

The pause felt like a lifetime, and Anouk knew even before her colleague spoke that the breathing that had been weak before was now absent. Instantly she began CPR.

The casualty had arrived in a bad way. How the crew had even got her from the scene of the explosion to the hospital without losing her was a testament to them, but she could tell this wasn't likely to go the way she would want. And she hated that. She hated losing a patient.

Any patient. Every *patient*.

She knew in this case she was fighting the inevitable, but did it matter? As long as she fought for the young woman lying in front of her?

She completed several rounds of CPR before her head finally reined in her heart.

'Pulse check?'

Even as her colleagues were checking one source, she was checking another.

'No pulse.'

No, not for her either. Anger and frustration coursed through Anouk as she lifted her head to the clock and announced the time of death.

'We didn't stand a chance,' one of her colleagues muttered, tapping her lightly on the shoulder as she passed.

Anouk dipped her head. Much as she knew that, it didn't always help. She reached for the curtains. There wasn't time to stop and grieve; the casualties were coming in thick and fast. No sooner would she step out than there would be another emergency to deal with.

Normally this was what she thrived on—not the losses, of course, but the challenge, the wins, the lives saved. But tonight there were too many other fears racing around her brain, and not all to do with Sol.

In some ways she was almost grateful for the distraction. Perhaps she'd been impulsive thinking that she could have a one-night stand with Sol. With anyone. Maybe it was a good thing they hadn't ended up back at his apartment. At least now she had time to think and realise what a bad decision that would have been.

Wouldn't it?

So why could she only think about surrendering to the temptation that had been haunting her ever since their intimate encounter?

Her head was reeling.

She told herself it was the fear of knowing that the explosion was so close to her and Saskia's apartment block. She'd tried calling her friend on the way to the hospital, but it had gone straight to voicemail. She had no way of knowing if Saskia was all right. Or even where she was.

So that was definitely a concern. But it wasn't what filled her mind with such a confusion of thoughts.

No, she suspected that tangle was more to do with the man who she would have been with, *right now*, if that accident hadn't happened.

It was why she needed a good save more than anything. She needed Saskia and she needed the high of saving lives to push the unwelcome thoughts of Sol from her brain. Given the emergencies flooding in, and not enough staff yet able to get to the hospital, there was plenty for her to do.

As the porters dealt with the deceased patient in the bay, Anouk pushed the loss out of her head and moved on to the next bay, only for Sol to catch her before she went in.

For an instant her heart jolted madly and everything seemed to come into sharper focus.

'What are you doing here?'

'Someone paged Neuro,' he replied evenly. 'A thirty-two-year-old cyclist with T12 and L1 fractures?'

'That's one of my cases.' Whatever her body might be feeling, her brain flipped immediately, locking back into professional mode. 'In here.'

He followed her quickly into a bay, nodding a brief greeting to the girl who was sitting, terrified, at the bedside of her injured boyfriend.

'This is Jared,' Anouk told Sol. 'He came in earlier and we've already had him up to CT.'

'He was caught in the blast?'

'Yes, we understood from witnesses who spoke to the air ambulance team that Jared went over the handlebars and was thrown into another vehicle. He was wearing a crash helmet. The head to pelvis CT scan showed fractured third and fourth ribs with a right-sided pneumothorax. Fractured T12 and L1 with possible evidence of neuro-compromise. He had a deep gash on his right thigh, which we have dealt with. He's had a total of around fourteen mils morphine.'

'Understood,' Sol agreed. 'I need to look at the imaging and decide what to do about the spine.'

'Agreed. I was working on the basis that if he has broken vertebrae at T12 and L1 there are likely to be depressional fractures through the endplates.'

It shouldn't have surprised her how well, how slickly, the two of them were working together. Almost as if the gala evening had never happened.

'Get it to me,' confirmed Sol, already jogging to his next call.

Little wonder the demand on the neuro team would be ridiculously high tonight.

* * *

For several hours Anouk worked steadily, hurrying between patients. She struggled to find beds for the unending stream of casualties injured in the blast. Still, she hadn't realised how much time had passed until she dashed from her current patient in order to call Neuro again, only for Sol to appear as she lifted the receiver.

'I've just been looking for you.'

'Thank goodness.' Dropping down the receiver, Anouk pulled a grimace as she turned to him. 'I thought no one was going to be able to get here.'

'About Jared? The cyclist with the T12 and L1 fractures?'

'Sorry?'

'I'm satisfied that the fractures are stable and that no intervention by us is necessary. I'm also confident that there is no neuro deficit so you can admit him to trauma team care, but he doesn't need to be transferred to Neuro.'

'Right.' Anouk hailed one of the nurses to relay the message and ensure the transfer happened quickly to free up a precious resus bed, simultaneously grabbing Sol's lapels as he made to move away.

'Anouk?' he growled as he swung back to her, his dark gaze taking in her hands still gripping his clothing.

She didn't even have time to feel abashed.

'I need you to look at this patient. It's urgent.'

'I came down to give you the results. I have another patient to see. You're probably on Ali's list—she'll be on her way as soon as she's finished with her patient upstairs.'

'There isn't time to wait for Ali.' Anouk shook her head, ushering him to the screen and calling up a new set of images.

Vaguely, it occurred to her that he could have objected. He could have focussed on his next assigned patient, but he was trusting her that this was critical.

'Her name is Jocelyn,' Anouk explained, still bringing up the images. 'She was right outside the building when the explosion occurred and the blast wave knocked her across the road and into a wall. She had a loss of consciousness for approximately ten minutes. On arrival of paramedics she had a GCS of three, which transitioned to a GCS of eleven. Very aggressive and we have confirmed with her husband that it's out of character. The patient was put into a medically induced coma and taken to CT.'

She flashed the images up on the screen.

'A large extradural haematoma.' Sol pursed his lips. 'Very large, in fact.'

'Yes,' Anouk agreed. 'Midline shift.'

'And it has shifted more?' he confirmed.

'Yes.'

They both knew that immediate surgery was imperative. Best case would be that the neurosurgeons could drain the blood and that the brain could move back into place and heal over. Most likely it would never be the same, but the faster they moved, the more chance there was.

Worst case, Jocelyn would die.

'I'll take her,' Sol confirmed after verifying the images for himself. 'I'll push my patient to Ali—he isn't as critical.'

'Thanks.'

With a nod, Sol straightened and moved away quickly, and Anouk couldn't help feeling warm.

She could pretend it was because she knew that her patient was in the very best hands. But she knew that wasn't all it was.

The night flew by, exhausting and chaotic, but with enough saves to bolster Anouk and her team as twelve hours went by, then eighteen, then twenty-four and the casualties had finally thinned out, the wail of ambulances subsiding.

And Anouk could finally go home. She tried not to think of where she might have been now if the gas explosion had never happened. Would she still be at Sol's, or would he have found a way to subtly eject her from his apartment rather than have her stay the night? Somehow, she couldn't imagine it. Playboy or not, it just didn't seem… *Sol-like.*

Then again, what was she doing imagining *anything*?

She rounded the corner, straight into Saskia. They had seen each other in Resus, passing as they darted into different bays but, incredibly, their cases hadn't coincided all evening. But now, without even uttering a word, her friend hugged her tightly.

'I was so relieved when I heard you were safe.'

'Why wouldn't I be?' Anouk laughed. 'And never mind me, the hospital is practically buzzing with some gossip that you arrived by helicopter?'

Saskia thrust her away, her eyes searching Anouk.

'You haven't heard, then?' Saskia demanded, ignoring the comment.

A sense of unease began to creep through Anouk.

'Heard what?'

'That the explosion affected Kings Boulevard?'

'That's us.' Anouk frowned.

'Yes. The whole area has been cordoned off until they can determine which buildings are structurally intact and which aren't. We can't go home.' Anouk couldn't answer as Saskia hugged her again. 'At least we're both safe.'

'We should…book a hotel, then.' Anouk fought off the daze that had settled over her. 'I'll call now.'

'Not for me.' Her friend placed her hand over Anouk's as she reached into her locker for her mobile. 'I'm… I have somewhere to be.'

'Where?'

'I… I'm staying with Malachi,' Saskia apologised.

'With Malachi?'

Sol's brother?

It didn't make much sense but Saskia was already changing her shoes and closing her bag.

'Saskia? Are you in here?' Sol's voice only seemed to ramp up the tension in the room.

Or perhaps it was just her, Anouk thought, flustered.

'Oh, Anouk.' Was it her imagination or did he pause for a fraction of a second when he spotted her, before addressing Saskia again? 'Mal says you need to get going. His heli is on the roof and they want it cleared in case an emergency has to come in.'

'I should go,' Saskia muttered.

Sol looked at her.

'If you're calling for a hotel, Anouk, you're too late. I heard a couple of guys complaining an hour ago that every hotel in the city was booked out. The cordon is quite extensive—lots of apartment blocks have been evacuated.'

'Great.' She gritted her teeth as Saskia hovered, still not leaving. Worry etched in her face.

'You could find an on-call room.'

'I'm guessing they'll be taken, too,' Sol told them. 'They're setting up temporary beds in community centres around the place.'

'Oh,' Anouk bit out as Saskia grabbed her hand.

'I could speak to Malachi? See if you could come with us?'

'Or you could just stay with me,' Sol cut in, quietly, firmly.

He didn't finish the sentence. He didn't need to. It hung there, in the silence between them.

She could stay with Sol...*as she had been going to do before the explosion had happened.*

Only it wasn't twenty-odd hours ago and things had shifted since that reckless moment in the coffee shop. That moment had gone. They could pretend it was just exhaustion from the chaotic shift; she would be happy with that.

'Thanks, but I don't think it's a good idea.'

They both knew what she meant by it. But her objection was drowned out by her friend who, Anouk was sure, cast Sol a grateful look.

'That's a great idea.'

What was going on here?

'I'm sorry, I do have to go,' Saskia muttered, squeezing her hand again.

'I don't understand, Sask?'

'It's complicated. I'll explain everything when I can.'

Then Saskia hurried out of the room, leaving Anouk staring as the door closed behind her friend. The flashback to her teenage years was as sudden as it was unexpected. The moment she'd first realised that people were moving on whilst she was standing still. Too caught up in her mother's dramas to have time for a life of her own.

Was it possible she'd been standing still ever since?

'Do you know what that was about?' she asked Sol before she could stop herself.

He shoved his hands into his pockets and leaned back against the wall. He looked ridiculously model-like. And dammit if a thrilling shiver didn't dance down her spine.

'Possibly.'

'But you aren't going to tell me?'

'I don't know anything for sure.' He shrugged. 'When they want us to know, they'll tell us.'

'There's a *they*?'

She wasn't surprised when he didn't elaborate.

'I don't believe it's my business,' he said calmly. 'Now, do you want a place to stay or not?'

He just waited calmly, as though offering her a place to stay when there was nowhere else was no big deal. Yet she wouldn't take it, not because she was afraid of what might happen between them, but because she was afraid that she *wanted* it too much.

And if it did, what was the worst that could happen? They'd enjoy a night, maybe a few nights, of intimacy. Even the memory of that night at the gala was enough to have her... *aching.* Just as she'd been ever since.

And hadn't she already considered that maybe it was a good thing she hadn't ended up at his house twenty-four hours ago? That maybe it was *fate*?

Maybe that argument had worked when her mind had been preoccupied by her patients. Her job. Only now the ready-made excuse was gone, it seemed that she wasn't as eager to head somewhere alone, after all. Not when Sol was standing, in all his six-three, honed glory in front of her.

Not when he'd acted as a dashing knight in blue scrubs on several occasions for her patients tonight.

'What happened to Jocelyn?' she demanded abruptly.

'Two hours in surgery. We'll keep her in an induced coma for the next few days and see what happens when she wakes up.'

'And then you take it from there?'

He lifted a shoulder in acknowledgement.

Nothing was certain in this life. But if it had been a test as to whether he cared enough about his patients to know their names, he had passed. With flying colours.

She was going home with him. It was inexorable.

'I'm not one of your conquests.' The words spilled out before she could stop them. 'That is, I'm only agreeing to this if you promise me that no one will find out.'

'Agreeing to *this*?' he challenged, his face a picture of innocence.

She sucked in a deep breath and quelled her irritation.

'You know what I'm saying.'

'I don't believe that I do.' He raised his eyebrows but amusement tugged at that sinful mouth. 'Elucidate.'

Anouk huffed.

But if she couldn't even say the word then how was she going to manage to do it?

'Casual sex,' she clarified stiffly.

'Indeed?' He grinned wolfishly and she felt it like teeth against her soul. 'Forgive me if I'm wrong, but I seem to recall simply offering you a place to stay since there was nowhere else. I don't recall sex ever being a detail of the discussion.'

Heat flooded her body.

'I… You…' She faltered, hardly able to believe her own *faux pas*.

What was it about Sol that had her acting so out of character? So recklessly? First at the gala, and now *this*. Shame chased through her, and then something else.

It took her a moment to realise that it was anger. She grabbed hold of it. At least it gave her a sense of courage, even if it was a false sensation.

'You're right, you didn't. I assumed,' she ground out. 'But then, we both know that's where we will end up. Look where we were headed before we got called in last night.'

'I seem to remember you muttering something about it being a sign.' He smirked. 'Though personally, I've never believed in that nonsense.'

'No, you told me as much,' she reminded him crossly. 'You also told me that it was inevitable. That however much I tried to outrun it, it would catch up with me sooner or later and topple me to the ground. That the faster and further I ran, the fall would be all the harder as a result.'

'I didn't realise you were paying such close attention to every word I was saying.' Sol stretched his legs out languorously. 'Not that I am complaining, you understand.'

'You're playing games aren't you?' she realised, disappointment plummeting through her.

The air around them turned cooler in an instant, as Sol pushed himself off the wall.

'Contrary to the low opinion you hold about me, Anouk, I don't play games every moment of every conversation.'

'Common consensus is that you do,' she rallied.

She wasn't sure what else to do, his reaction was so unexpected. As though she'd hit a nerve, even though she'd never known him to have a nerve when it came to the way he revelled in his reputation. So obviously that couldn't be right.

'You're right,' he managed flatly, moving past her and heading for the door. 'But let's just say that it has been a long, exhausting twenty-four hours, and frankly I'm too weary for game-playing.'

'I see.' Not seeing at all, Anouk grabbed her bag and hurried after him.

Actually, he did look rather...out of character.

'So, for tonight at least, you're safe. All I'm offering you is a place to sleep and nothing more. We'll have to walk; the car is still by the new carers' centre. Does that suit you?'

'Perfectly,' she confirmed. Lying through her teeth.

CHAPTER NINE

'DID SOMETHING HAPPEN with one of your patients?' she ventured after they'd been walking for a while.

'Why?'

'Because you're acting...differently. And I think I get that way, every now and again, when one particular patient gets under my skin.'

He slowed, but didn't stop.

'It was, wasn't it?' she pressed him gently.

They continued walking in silence. Everywhere oddly quiet after weathering that storm in the hospital.

'A baby boy. Nineteen months,' was all Sol said, after what seemed like an age.

She didn't answer. Instead she simply fell into step with him, and hoped that it was enough. She understood only too well.

It was another age before he spoke again.

'It's odd, the way it gets to you sometimes,

don't you think?' he said, his head down and his hands thrust into his pockets.

The question was more rhetorical than anything, Anouk knew that, but she answered anyway.

'You mean loss? Death?'

'We deal with it every day. It's so easy to become desensitised to it.' He shrugged. 'But after an incident like that...'

'Yes,' she whispered. 'I think it's the sheer volume of it. All at once. It makes it feel too much.'

Again, they walked in companionable silence for minutes—though it felt like a lifetime, lost as she was in her thoughts. It was only when he stopped at a shop window that she realised they had made it to the lower part of the town. Slowing down, she backed up, but she wasn't prepared.

'What is this, Sol?'

'You asked me about the Christmas village scene.'

'This is it?'

'This is it.'

She turned to take in the scene. Even through her loathing of this time of year, she could at least admit it was spectacular. Little trains ran in circles around the quaintest village set-up; a snow-covered village green with tiny figures walking, ice-skating, or simply strolling the wintry streets in the warm glow of the orange/yellow lights.

Little old-fashioned shops lined the painstakingly constructed hillside road, which, if she looked closely, Anouk thought might be polystyrene blocks, but they looked for all the world like snowy inclines. Meanwhile, a miniature cable car ran up and down another polystyrene hill scene.

'This is what the kids work so hard to raise the money to buy,' Anouk murmured. 'For you, and for Malachi. Why?'

There was a beat of silence.

'Why, Sol?' She pressed her fingers to the glass, as if proximity could solve the riddle she was sure existed.

'It's become a tradition,' he offered simply.

'What makes it so traditional?' she repeated.

There was no logical explanation for why it should matter to her to know.

Yet it did.

The still night began to hum with anticipation.

She turned her head to watch him but his gaze was fixed on the scene, not on her.

'Please, Sol?

He scowled, drawing in a deep breath before answering.

'Malachi and I were kids when we first saw a village like this,' he began, falteringly at first. He hadn't told this story in…well, ever. 'There was a toyshop in town which had one every Christmas—not that we were ever allowed in, of course. The owner would chase us down the road if we even peered into the window, for steaming it up with our snotty noses.'

'He really said that?'

'He said a sight worse than that. Even clipped our legs with the back of a broom handle on more than one occasion.' Sol shrugged. 'Anyway, sometimes we would wait until it was dark and sneak out of the house if we could leave Mum for long enough. There was a guy with a sugared doughnut stall and if he was still there cleaning up, he used to give us any leftovers, which would otherwise get thrown away.'

'That's nice.' Anouk smiled as though her chest was tight and painful at the thought of Sol's childhood.

She'd had no idea. But then, no one did. Clearly that was the way Sol liked it.

'He was a decent guy. Years later, when Mal had made his first real money as a boxer, he bought the business from the guy for about five times its worth, just to repay him.'

'Did he know?'

'Yeah, he was so damned grateful, it was really nice to do. Mal then gave the business to a couple of kids he knew would appreciate it, from the first centre we built. They ended up getting four stalls between them and they're still going strong.'

'Wow.'

She thought Sol was going to say more but suddenly he caught himself. As if he didn't know why he'd told her that. Possibly it had all been stuffed down in the same box for so many years that now she'd sprung the lid, random snippets were springing out left and right, completely out of his control and in no logical order.

Or maybe he was just playing her.

'Anyway. Mal and I used to sneak down to watch the little trains going around, and the carousel, and the people going in and out of buildings on that turntable. And we vowed that we would make it through to the other side and we'd buy every damned piece of that village in existence. We swore we'd become the kind of people who idiots like that toyshop owner would fawn over. Never again would we get chased from a shop doorway or window.'

'You guys must have had the kind of money to buy a village *world* years ago. Several times over. But you didn't?' Anouk eyed him thoughtfully. The deep blue pools were fathoms deep.

'We did, as it happens.' He smiled a genuine smile. 'We bought the lot. Just to know what it felt like.'

'And?'

'And it felt good.' He laughed suddenly. 'A bit surreal, that first time we set it up. Young adults reliving a childhood moment that had once been denied them. But after that we felt like we'd made our point, if only to ourselves. So we split it out and sent a bundle to each of about five or six kids' community centres.'

'And one of them was Care to Play?' Anouk guessed.

'Yeah. Once the kids there found out, they decided that was what they wanted to do for us, buy a new piece every year. It's a matter of pride to them, to do something to raise money for a new toyshop, or ride, or ice-skating rink.'

'That's really nice.' She glanced around rue-fully. 'Even I bought into the idea. I thought you'd love this, but you just do it for the kids.'

'Why not? They get pleasure from it, too.'

'That's another thing which confused me,' she admitted. 'At the centre you're an inspiration for making good from nothing. At the hospital, the rumour is that you both came from money?'

'At the hospital it's just that,' he growled. 'A rumour. Malachi has become a multimillionaire thanks to his boxing, but I'm not.'

'You must earn a decent salary as a neurosurgeon?'

He raised an eyebrow at her.

'Did I say I was complaining?'

'Well, no,' she conceded. 'So why not just tell people that?'

'Why bother? It isn't any of their business and because it would invite questions, more interest, delving into my past—and Malachi's.'

'Surely that's a good thing? Two boys, with humble beginnings, have done incredibly well for themselves. It's the fairy tale, people would have lapped it up. You'd have had even more women falling at your feet.'

She hadn't intended to sound so cross when she'd made that latter observation.

'I told you,' he cut across her, 'it would have been an invitation for people to rifle through our lives like they're some kind of public property.'

Surprisingly, Anouk was beginning to realise just how protective both Sol, and particularly Malachi, were about their private lives.

Who would have thought it?

But she couldn't ask anything more, she didn't dare. Not after he'd effectively shut down that line of conversation. And still, his gaze held hers and she couldn't move. He might not have told her a lot, but, given his driving need for privacy, she felt as though he'd told her more than she could have hoped he would.

As though she was significant.

'Did you know that ridiculous pudding hat of yours was on inside out?' he told her, lifting it gently and turning it right side out before lowering it back on her head. Infinitely tender, infinitely thrilling.

She waited, pinned to the spot, as he released

her hat and cupped her face instead, like a blast of heat in the cold winter air.

'Sol?' she breathed, when neither of them had moved and it was clear that neither of them was going to move.

Still, they both remained motionless. And then, just when Anouk had finished telling herself that she had to be the one to step back, to break the contact, however much she railed against it, he bent his head and brushed her lips with his.

It ignited a fire in an instant, sending the surrounding people, the coffee shop, the entire street, reeling into the background.

With a low moan, she stepped towards him, her arms raised to grab his jacket with her hands. Whether she deepened the kiss or Sol did, it hardly mattered.

His mouth was hot and demanding, his taste every bit as exhilarating as she remembered. It confirmed the one truth she'd suspected since the gala ball—one night with him hadn't been enough. She wanted more. She *needed* more.

He kissed her with ruinous skill, turning her inside out and upside down. He plundered and claimed, teasing her with his lips, his tongue, his teeth; he pulled her body to him until she was sure she could feel every last muscled ridge of that washboard body that had stamped itself so indelibly in her mind, and he made a low sound as he kissed her as if, like her, he needed more.

And she was lost. As enchanted by the man as every other woman before her had been.

She who should know better.

'My place?' he broke contact long enough to mutter.

Anouk didn't even try to speak, she just nodded.

They barely even made it through the door of his apartment before they were undressing each other.

Sol's touch was fire over every millimetre of her skin, smouldering over her wherever he trailed those expert fingers of his. Setting her ablaze every time he lowered his head, and that skilful mouth, to brand her somewhere new.

Her neck, her shoulder, the rise of her breast. One hand laced itself through her hair, cupping the nape of her neck and making her feel cherished and precious, whilst the other hand played a wicked concerto on her body as if it were the most exquisite instrument.

And with every accomplished stroke the fire inside her grew hotter and brighter, until it was too painful to look at. And so Anouk closed her eyes and gave herself over to the sheer beauty of it. She was singing in her head, arias she had never known before. Certainly not like this.

Again and again Sol moved his fingers, his hand, his mouth, over her body, testing her and tasting her. Paying homage to every inch of her, he supported her neck with one hand while the other skimmed over her back and then spanned the hollow at the base of her spine with enviably long, strong fingers, making her feel infinitely delicate.

He took his time, as though they were in no rush. As though there was no end goal, trailing his fingers up one side and down again, leaving shivers of delight in his wake.

Up and down.

Up again, and down again.

Pleasing and punishing her, until every molecule of her pulsed with burning, intense need. All she could do was respond to him. As if she'd been waiting for this moment for ever. As if she were his to command.

As if she were *his*.

Time stood still for Anouk. She stayed there in his arms, letting all this desire swirl around, and move through her as Sol branded her with every touch, leaving her feeling as though she would never be the same again.

This is his skill, a tiny voice urged silently in her head. *He makes you feel special, unique, and as long as you don't fall for him, it will be fine.*

But the voice was too hazy, too muffled, too deliberately easy for the sensations tearing through her to drown out. Or perhaps it was more that she wanted to drown *in* the sensations. To drown in Sol.

It was only when she heard the loud, delectably rude sound of a zip sliding that she realised he had unfastened her jeans and was sliding his fingers under the material.

They hadn't even made it to the bedroom.

'Do you want to… I mean…here?' she began weakly, the words catching in her throat as, without warning, he brushed one finger tantalisingly over the front of her underwear.

Then the damned man lifted his head and shot her the most devilish grin.

'Sorry, what were you saying?'

But it was the dark, oddly intent look in his

eyes that snagged at her the most. As though he wasn't quite as in control as he wanted to appear. As if she was affecting him that little bit more than he wanted to reveal.

It was a heady thought. And then, before she could find her voice, he hooked the material back and repeated the action, this time with no barrier between them.

'Did you want me to stop?'

There was no mistaking the rawness in his voice just then, but before she could answer he let his fingers move over her, stroking her once, twice, before dipping into her heat.

Everything in her clenched in delicious anticipation. But then her eyes flew open as he drew his hand back up, and she was powerless to prevent a small sound of objection from escaping her lips.

'Relax,' he commanded, his tone purely hedonistic. 'I'm not going anywhere. Except here.'

And before she could say a word he lifted his finger to his mouth and licked it. Very deliberately.

'What…' she managed to find her voice, as jagged as it sounded '…are you doing?'

He fixed her with a lazy, hooded look.

'Tasting you.' His voice was thick, loaded. 'And you are as intoxicating as I remember.'

She had no idea how she managed to speak; her whole body was jolting with need.

'You've been remembering this?'

'Yes,' he growled, sliding his hand back into her trousers and his cool, wet finger straight over where she needed him most. 'And I've been imagining a hell of a lot more. So, let me ask you again, shall I continue or did you want me to stop?'

Her eyes fluttered slightly and it was all Anouk could do to bite her lip and shake her head. He'd stolen her voice again with a flick of his fingers, as if he were some wicked sorcerer using his clever fingers to wind the most magical of spells around her.

'Say it,' he growled.

It was an effort to open her heavy eyelids. Even more of one to speak. So instead she lifted her bottom, just a fraction, to brush his hand.

Yet it seemed he was one step ahead of her, and as she moved his hand shifted out of reach. Barely. She could still feel the heat from him rolling over her, but she couldn't make contact.

'I find I want to hear the words from you,' Sol ground out.

The man was a fiend!

She swallowed. Hard.

'Continue,' she managed hoarsely. 'Definitely, continue.'

Sol seemed only too happy to oblige.

'So wet,' he growled in a voice so carnal that it sent another ache slicing through her right to her core.

Anouk tried to answer, but speech was impossible. Even before he slid those expert fingers around to caress her.

It took her a moment to realise that the low moans she heard were her own. This—what Sol was doing to her right now—was like nothing she'd ever known before.

So adrift, so out of her own body, and yet so wholly at its mercy all at the same time. She was vaguely aware of moving her head so that she could fit her mouth back to Sol's, every slip and slide of his tongue mirroring what his fingers were doing, stoking that fire higher with each passing moment.

He moved his other hand from the nape of her neck to cup her cheek, cradling it almost tenderly, if she hadn't known that to be ridiculous. Still, when he angled his head for a deeper fit, she poured more into that kiss than she'd ever known possible.

It was incredible, the sensations rushing through her body from her mouth to her core and back again, everywhere that Sol was; the devastating rhythm he was building inside her. She would be ruined for any other man. She was sure of it. Solomon Gunn would make sure that no other man would ever be able to satisfy her again.

She didn't think she cared—just as long as he never stopped doing what he was doing now.

She sighed, a sound of deep longing, causing Sol to wrench his mouth from hers, his eyes seeking her out and staring at her as though trying to see something in them. Either that, or conveying some silent message that she couldn't understand. She wanted to ask him, but it wasn't in her to speak, his dexterous fingers leaving her only just able to breathe; tracing her shape, holding her, cradling her and then, finally, slipping inside her slick heat. She felt the shudder roll through her even before she heard her needy moan.

His eyes went almost black with desire.

'You respond so perfectly, *zoloste*,' he murmured, his gravelly voice the perfect telltale.

She bit her lip and nodded, unable to speak. Not that it mattered, she wouldn't know what to say even if she could. His fingers were still moving over her, around her, inside her. And she couldn't get enough. Especially when he lowered his head, placing his wicked mouth on her neck and driving her wild with his clever tongue and devilish teeth.

She didn't know when she began moving against his palm, urging him to quicken the pace when he seemed to want to take it at his own leisurely pace—to stretch out the blissful agony in her that much longer—she only knew she could feel herself hurtling along, and the abyss coming up on her so quickly she thought she might hurtle down for ever and ever and ever.

And she wanted Sol inside her. Properly. She reached down his body to his belt buckle, her fingers fumbling in her haste. She could feel him. Steel straining behind the denim, as though he wanted her just as badly. It was a thrilling thought. If only she could work the damned belt.

The driving rhythm didn't stop or even slow

for an instant, but with his free hand Sol caught her wrists and moved her away.

'There's time enough for that,' he muttered, every word dancing across her skin as his fingers continued their devastating concerto. 'Right now, this is about you.'

She'd never felt so worshipped, so powerful, or so confident in her own body.

Finally it broke over her, as if every nerve ending in her entire body were fizzing and popping, from the top of her head right down to her very toes, and then he twisted his wrist skilfully, in a way she'd never known before, and she felt herself catapult into the air. Higher and higher, further and longer, soaring spectacularly on a wave of shimmering, magical sensation that she thought might never end.

She certainly never wanted it to. And still Sol touched her, held her. So that as the wave finally began to slow, and drop, she found herself tumbling straight onto another, which took her soaring back up again.

Time after time.

Finally, sated and spent, she felt herself tumbling, her body sagging into Sol's, her breathing rapid and harsh.

And all she could do was hope that he broke her fall when she finally hit the ground.

Anouk was in his bed by the time she started coming back to herself. Right where he'd been imagining her for too long now. As nonsensical as that notion was. He watched her, half amused, half ravenous, as she blinked and tried to focus on her new surroundings.

'Oh.' The small sound escaped her lips and he was powerless to do anything but lower his head and try to catch the sound in his own mouth.

'I took the liberty of bringing you to my bed,' he managed. Then, as her eyes wandered down to his naked form, he added, 'I also took the liberty of stripping. Is that a problem?'

'On the contrary.' Her voice was thick, hoarse, and he liked that she couldn't conceal her need for him. 'I find I rather like that.'

And then, as if to prove her point, she stretched beneath him, parting her legs to settle him against her wet heat, and Sol almost lost it there and then.

'There's no rush, *zolotse*,' he chided gently, as though he himself weren't so perilously close to the edge.

But then Anouk looped her arms around his neck and her legs around his body and shot him a daring, cheeky grin.

'Are you quite sure about that?'

Before he could answer, she lifted her hips and drew him inside her, as taut, scorching need knotted in his belly.

It stole his breath from his very lungs.

With a low moan, he thrust inside her, revelling in her answering shudder. The way she locked her legs tighter around him, and lifted her hips to meet him. He made himself slide out of her slowly, then back in again, setting a deliberate pace and fighting the driving urge to take her there and then.

He had no idea how he kept it going. Whether he even managed it for long at all. But then he found he was moving faster, harder, deeper, and Anouk was matching him stroke for stroke. And he could feel it building inside her, just as it was inside him.

When her breath came in shallower gasps, he hooked his hand under her and angled her perfectly, reaching between them to find the very centre of her need, and then he sent her over the edge, the sound of her crying his name far more potent than it should have been.

And Sol, unable to bear it any longer, followed her.

CHAPTER TEN

HE KNEW SHE was gone even before his eyes had adjusted to the pitch-black of the room. He could sense it. The bed felt...empty without her. And an irrational sense of anger rolled through him that she should have snuck out, like some kind of thief, whilst he slept. He who never slept soundly.

Throwing back the sheet and stabbing his legs into a pair of night-time joggers, he stomped out of the bedroom and down the hallway. And stopped abruptly.

The light to the living area was on and he could hear the sound of cutlery on porcelain. It was insane how glad that sound made him.

Wandering through, he leaned on the door-jamb and watched her, perched on the granite worktop, one of his T-shirts swamping her delectable body, eating his cereal.

'Hungry?'

She jumped instantly.

'It was a long shift and…an energetic night.' She offered him a sheepish grin. 'I didn't mean to wake you.'

'You didn't.'

Stepping in, he opened the cupboards and retrieved his own cereal bowl, filling it up and pouring on the milk she had left on the counter, before putting the bottle away.

'I didn't realise you were a neat freak,' she teased.

'I didn't consider that you were a slob.' He laughed.

She straightened up indignantly.

'I am not, I was going to clean up as soon as I'd finished, so you can take that back.'

'Fair enough.' He took a spoonful of the cereal, watching her wriggle off the counter-top and potter around his kitchen.

He had no idea what rippled through him at the sight but he didn't care to analyse it too deeply.

'So…do I come back to…your bed? Or do I… go to the guest room?'

Ah, so the new, bold Anouk had taken cover again and the old, reserved Anouk was back.

'Come back to bed.' He didn't even bother to keep the amusement from his tone.

'It's all very well for you to laugh.' She bristled. 'But I'm not used to...*this*.'

'I know I have a reputation as a playboy, Anouk. But I'm not a complete bastard. Just because I'm not cut out for relationships, or love, or any of that mumbo jumbo, doesn't mean I throw women out in the middle of the night as soon as the sex is over.'

'About that,' Anouk announced, loudly if a little shakily. 'I think that's utter tosh, as it happens.'

'Say that again?'

To say he was incredulous didn't cut it. Anouk moistened her lips nervously and he had to force himself not to let his eyes linger.

'I think you use sex as a distraction,' she declared.

'Is that so?'

'Yes.' Clearly warming to her subject, she drew herself a little taller and eyed him determinedly. 'I think you use sex as a distraction to stop you from getting too close to anyone.'

Anger and something else—something someone who didn't know him might have categorised as fear—spread through his mind.

'This idea that you're not cut out for relation-ships, or love is nonsense.'

'Careful, *zoloste*, you're wandering into pre-carious territory.'

A lesser woman would have backed away at the dangerous edge in his voice.

But then, Anouk wasn't a lesser anything.

'Someone has to,' defiance laced her tone.

'Why? Because you want me to tell you that I love you?'

'No!' she actually looked horrified. 'Not me. Of course not. That's...insane.'

'Of course it's insane,' Sol couldn't pinpoint what charged through him in that millisecond. He didn't want to. 'Because I'm not a man who believes in 'love'. I certainly can't offer it.'

'I think you *are* capable of love.' The panic was gone and her defiance was back again. 'The way you are with your patients, and those young carers, and even your relationship with your brother Malachi. You care, in everything that you do.'

He hated the way she thought he was a better man than he was. It only made it more apparent to him that he wasn't that man.

'You're trying to make me into something I'm

not to suit your own agenda, *zolotse*,' he gritted out, suddenly angry. Because anger was easier than these other emotions that threatened to churn inside him. 'Because you hate yourself for a one-night stand with me and you want to make yourself feel better by claiming I can be more than that. But that isn't me. I'm not built that way, Anouk. I don't want to be. I warned you about that.'

She hated hearing those words; he could see it in her stiff stance, and the belligerent tilt of her head.

'That isn't what I'm doing, Sol,' she snapped. 'I'm telling you that I think you're a different man from the image of yourself you put out there, and I don't know if it's because you want others to believe that's all there is to you, or if you actually really do believe it's the truth. But, whatever the truth is, that's for you to know. It has no bearing on me, either way.'

'Your eagerness to change me suggests otherwise.'

If his cereal had contained broken glass, it couldn't have shredded him inside any worse. But Anouk didn't reply straight away. She just watched him, a solemn expression in those arresting blue eyes.

He couldn't help wishing he knew what she was thinking.

'Did I ever tell you that the reason I came to the UK was to find my father?' she asked, just as he was about to give up thinking she was going to speak again.

They both knew the answer to that. Her eyes were too bright, too flitting. He doubted she'd ever told anyone, expect maybe Saskia. Still, he could play the game for her, if that was what she needed.

He realised his previous anger had begun to dissipate.

'No.' He feigned a casualness. 'I don't think you did.'

'Just before my mother…died…' she faltered '…she told me that she had once received a letter from my father.'

'You hadn't known him?'

'Not at all. Only the story she'd told me about him not wanting to be around for us.' Her strained tone suggested that wasn't all there was to it, but Sol didn't press her on it. It was shocking enough that she was telling him this much. 'I didn't know he'd ever contacted us. Her. Me.'

'What did he say?'

'I don't know.' She looked angry for a moment, but then smoothed it away quickly, efficiently. 'Apparently she'd thrown it on the fire in a pique of temper. By the time she'd changed her mind, most of it was gone. She just about managed to retrieve part of an address.'

'To his home in the UK?'

Anouk eyed him speculatively for several long moments. There was patently more to the story than she was willing to reveal to him. And he shouldn't be so desperate to know the truth. To understand it more.

He shouldn't be so wrapped up in the abridged version she was feeding him now. It shouldn't matter to him.

'You came all the way from America because he lives in the UK.'

'Not just the UK. Moorlands itself,' she bit out, at length.

That was why she'd come here?

'Did you track him down?' He couldn't help himself.

What the hell was it about this woman that slid, so devilishly slickly, under his skin?

An internal war waged within Sol and for seconds, minutes, maybe hours, he couldn't breathe. He had no idea what would win.

There was another pause, before she nodded.

'Eight years ago. With Saskia.'

'And?'

'He'd died about five years before that. There was a young family living in the house, but the neighbours confirmed it.'

'You're sure it was him.'

'There's no doubt about it, Sol.' She offered a wan smile. 'I even visited his grave.'

'I'm so sorry,' he told her sincerely.

What more was there to say?

She leaned on the counter, her arms folded defensively across her chest.

'I'm not after pity, Sol. I just wanted you to know that I wasn't telling you that I think you're capable of love because I want you to love *me*. I know our deal was just sex. It's the only reason I agreed to it, so I'm not about to change the rules now. I don't want love in my life either. I don't trust it. I never have.'

Some seething thing slunk around inside him.

But the anger wasn't directed *at* Anouk any more. Or himself. It was directed at those people who had never deserved her care in the first place. Who had hurt her. Who had destroyed something as fragile and precious as her trust in anyone who could love her.

'You trusted the wrong people,' he gritted out, realising that he wanted to reach out and pull her to him.

To tell her that she was beautiful, and caring, and lovable. Especially because it was only now occurring to him that she didn't know that for herself. How had he not seen that before? He was usually skilled at reading others.

'Of course, I trusted the wrong people,' she agreed flatly. 'But who would have thought that my mother and my grandmother were those wrong people? They lied to me my whole life. In the end I think my mother only told me the truth to get one final dig at me. To prove to me that she'd had the upper hand right up until her moment of death.'

'That doesn't mean you should still let her get to you now. You can trust people. You can trust me.'

Her eyebrows shot up.

'Said the spider to the fly.'

It was a fair point. Maybe that was why it grated on him. Maybe that was why, instead of shutting her question down as he would have done had any other woman asked, he found himself answering the question she'd once put to him.

'I was five when Malachi started to become a carer.'

She blinked.

'You don't have to do this, Sol. I wasn't telling you about me just to make you feel obliged to do the same.'

'He became a carer for me, and for our mum, when she needed it,' he continued, as if she hadn't spoken.

She only hesitated for a moment.

'She was ill?'

If you could call being a drug addict ill. Some people called it an illness. Having lived through it, borne the brunt of it, he and Malachi had always been considerably less charitable. Not that Sol was about to say any of that aloud.

'Something like that.' He tried not to spit it out in distaste.

Clearly he didn't do a very good job; the expression on her face said enough. Less shock, more a tired understanding. As though she hadn't expected it from him, but, now that he'd said it, she wasn't entirely surprised.

Or maybe he was just projecting. This woman made him rethink things of which he'd long since stopped taking notice. He blinked as he realised she was still talking to him.

'Sol? I asked about your dad.'

'Dead. That's why she became...ill.'

'So he cared for you before that?' She was trying to put it together, like one of the jigsaws at the carers' centre, only it was a jigsaw of his life and he hadn't given her all the pieces.

With anyone else, he wouldn't have wanted to.

'*Cared* is a bit too generous a description,' Sol ground out. 'He was a former Russian soldier.'

'Your parents were Russian?'

'Not my mother,' he clarified. 'My father was medically discharged due to injury; he had street smarts but no education so he earned a living taking work on the docks when it was available, or as a pub fighter otherwise.'

'Did he hit you and Malachi?'

'No. He wasn't exactly the best father but he didn't hit us, except the odd clip around the ear as many kids got back them, not bad for a man who had been systematically used as a punching bag by his own father. Though he did teach us to fight, from toddlers really, but particularly Mal because he was older. It was his way of bonding with us, I guess.'

'So that's how Malachi became the skilled fighter he is now.'

'I doubt he'd ever have believed it would make Mal a millionaire.' Sol shook his head. 'Love wasn't something our father was good at. Even his relationship with our mother was more passionate and volatile than loving. She showed us some love as kids, and he put food on the table and a roof over our heads.'

'How did he die?'

'Bad fight.' Sol laughed but it was a hollow, scraping sound. 'Brain bleed. And yes, I know all the psychology arguments about that being the reason why I became a neurosurgeon. The point is that my mother fell apart. Started doing drugs to numb the pain. It wasn't a far reach from the world in which we lived back then. The love went pretty fast, then.'

'How old was Malachi?'

'Eight.' He shrugged as Anouk drew her lips

into a thin line. 'By the time he was ten, she was a full-on addict and Mal was full-time carer for us both, whilst he also earned money for us to eat and live.'

'He was earning money at ten?' Anouk blew out a breath. 'Doing what? Surely no one would employ him.'

'Local gangs.'

'Gangs?' She looked momentarily stunned. 'So…what did he do?'

Sol crossed his arms over his chest. Even now, over two decades on, it still rattled him that he didn't know exactly what his brother had been compelled to do just to keep the two—three— of them together.

Like holding their lives together with sticking plaster. No, not even something so expensive. His ten-year-old brother had been holding their lives together with a bit of discarded string he'd found blowing about in the filthy street outside their tiny terraced house.

He didn't even understand why he was telling Anouk any of this, and yet he couldn't seem to stop. She drew it out of him, with all the patience and compassion that he had used on the young carers in his centre.

It was odd, the tables being turned on him. And, strangely, not entirely unpleasant.

'Errands like drugs?' she pressed gently.

He emitted another harsh laugh. Given the state of their mother, drug gangs were people Malachi had never, ever worked for.

'No, never drugs. I don't know everything he did, you'd have to ask Mal, but things like being a runner for bookies. They trusted him because of our dad. Maybe he did things which were a bit dodgy but not outright illegal. Even as a kid Mal was always unshakeable on that.'

'He seems so quiet.' Anouk shook her head, evidently trying to absorb it all.

No judgement. No false sympathy or drama. Just...*her*. Listening. Caring. It should have concerned him more that he was letting her get so close, but he couldn't bring himself to back away. Even emotionally.

He told himself that he knew what he was doing.

'Mal isn't as quiet as people think. He has this inner core of steel, I'm telling you. Even as a kid he handled himself with those guys. Enough to make sure that I kept going to school. Believe it or not, I was always better with the discipline than he was.'

'Sol, the playboy, a good schoolboy?'

She offered him a soft smile and he realised she was teasing him. It was like a lick of heat.

'Amazing, isn't it?'

'So how did he get away with not going?'

'Mal has a true eidetic memory. He didn't really need to be in lessons to keep up with school. I used to…persuade some lads in his year to get copies of the work.'

'Persuade as in employ some of the fighting techniques your father had taught you?' she guessed.

'Only in the beginning.' Sol made no apologies. Not even to this woman. 'With those ten- or eleven-year-old lads who had trouble accepting a polite request from an eight-year-old. They rarely had trouble the next time.'

'I never realised.'

'Why would you?' Sol pointed out evenly. 'The point is that we got by, and if he hadn't done all of that I wouldn't have stayed in school, and without him I wouldn't be in medicine, let alone a neurosurgeon.'

Neither of them could have imagined even a

half of what they had today. Or just how far the two of them would pull themselves out of the gutter. Together. The way it had always been.

'What happened with your mum?'

He tensed; it was impossible not to.

'He got her the help she needed, but it turned out it still wasn't enough. She died when I was seventeen.'

'I'm sorry.'

'Don't be.' He shrugged, ignoring the odd scraping sensation deep inside his stomach. One that he was sure had more to do with the soft way that Anouk was looking at him than anything else. 'In some ways her death set Mal and me free.'

She stared at him for another long moment and he had to fight the urge to turn away lest she see right down to his soul. Down to where he still felt like that socially awkward, ashamed, inadequate kid.

'Is that where the playboy image came from? Not wanting to commit to someone, or settle down, or have kids because of your experience with your mum?'

Sol didn't answer.

He couldn't. Or wouldn't. Either way, the net result was the same.

He swung away to stare at the tiled wall, his hands resting on either side of him on the counter top. Behind him, he heard her slide off the granite surface. He could sense her approaching him and he turned, unable to help himself.

Suddenly they were facing each other, everything rending apart as Anouk placed her hands on either side of his face as if to make him look at her. He definitely didn't want to talk any more.

He forgot that he'd been doing all this to make her trust him. That he'd been waiting for her to need him so badly that she begged him, as she had the night of the gala.

'Confession time is over, *zolotse*,' he growled, snaking his arms to her waist and hauling her to him.

She didn't object. Especially not when he snagged her mouth with his.

Sol's whole body combusted in that one second. The woman was mouth-watering. Every slide of her tempting mouth, every shift of her delectable body, every tiny groan as he swept his finger over her sinfully hard nipples. He'd never *ached* so much before to bury himself inside a woman. Not aside from the primal, physi-cal urge, that was.

Anouk was dynamite where before he'd only known black powder.

CHAPTER ELEVEN

'WHAT IS THE matter with you, *bratik*?' Malachi challenged from across the expansive, luxury office just as Sol was filling his mug with hot, rich coffee from his brother's coffee maker.

'What?' Sol cocked an eyebrow, selecting a couple of Danish pastries to put onto a napkin and striding over to flop in a comfortable chair.

The last week had been unparalleled. So much for a one-night stand. He hadn't wanted to let Anouk go and she had been more than happy to stay. There hadn't been a room in his penthouse they hadn't used as their personal playground.

'You're full of the joys of spring,' sniped Malachi.

'And you're grouchy and on edge.' Sol eyed him shrewdly. 'More so than usual, that is. Though I wouldn't have thought that was possible.'

'Funny,' Malachi bit out.

'Thanks.'

'Idiot.'

Sol shrugged, wholly unconcerned, and wolfed down the second pastry before speaking again.

'Hungry by any chance?'

'Always.' Sol grinned, glancing around the room.

'*Vkusno!* So, what's the Christmas tree all about?'

He didn't think he'd ever seen so much as a bauble in his brother's offices before. Only Anouk had been more resistant to festive decorations than his brother always had been. Sol didn't know why, but he found himself staring at it a little harder. It looked remarkably similar to the one in Resus. The one that Anouk had said her friend Saskia had decorated.

He practically heard the clang as the penny hit the floor of his brain.

'I realised it's good for morale,' Malachi sidestepped. 'I'm not the only one who works here, you know. Listen, I've got a board meeting to prepare for, so do you want to tell me why you really schlepped across town to see me?'

Sol stared at his brother wordlessly. That tree had nothing to do with morale; it was about Saskia, plain and simple. Suddenly, he wondered if she was doing for Malachi anything like what Anouk was doing for him. Making him feel whole when he hadn't before recognised how broken he'd been? And, if so, didn't they all deserve this chance?

'You and I have always said that we weren't built for commitment, or love. That everything *she* put us through destroyed that in us. But what if we're wrong, Mal? What if you and I have always been capable of love?'

'This discussion is over,' Malachi ground out. But still, he didn't move.

'There's always been a love between you and me.' What had Anouk said? 'It may be a different kind of love, but it's love nonetheless.'

'Where did those pearls of wisdom come from?' Malachi snorted, but Sol noted that it lacked the level of scorn he might have expected from his big brother. He also noticed that Malachi wasn't outright dismissing him.

Or was he just reading too much into it because of the way Anouk had made him reevaluate his own priorities?

'I don't know,' he answered honestly.

'A woman?'

'No,' he denied. Then, 'Maybe.'

'Anouk?'

Reality bit hard, and for a moment Sol thought about denying it. What if talking about her with Malachi spoiled what he and Anouk had? *Might* have. Not that he even knew what they were— these...*feelings* that sloshed around inside him like sand and cement and water in a mixer.

'Are you going to take the proverbial?' He glowered at Malachi.

Their brotherly banter was inevitable, joshing each other, but for a moment, Malachi didn't say anything.

'Maybe next time.'

That was unexpected.

'Yeah, then,' Sol admitted. 'Anouk.'

'Something is going on between you both?'

Malachi didn't need to spell out that 'something going on' meant more than just him and Anouk having sex. His brother had mocked him for his playboy reputation plenty of times in the past.

'I don't know. Maybe.'

'Serious?'

Was it? If it wasn't, would he even be here? Doing this for her? He didn't care to examine that too deeply.

'Maybe. She's the reason I came here today, at least.'

His brother studied him, cool and perceptive.

'What do you need?' Malachi asked at length.

'You have people who can track stuff down for you, right?'

Malachi inclined his head.

'I want you to track down all you can on this man.' Sol flicked through his phone and found the notepad where he'd copied down the details from the scrap of paper in Anouk's picture frame, leaning forward to spin it across the desk to his brother. 'He died thirteen years ago, but he used to live there.'

Wordlessly, Malachi read the screen and made a note of the information. He didn't even question it and, not for the first time, Sol wondered how different his life would have been if he hadn't had his brother.

Anouk was right. Their relationship with their mother might have been destructive and damaging, but the two brothers had always believed in each other, loved each other. In their own fierce way.

How was it that she—a relative stranger—had

understood even when he hadn't really been able to see it? He doubted Malachi had either.

What was that saying about not seeing the wood for the trees?

'Do you think you can do this without hurting her, Sol?' Malachi demanded suddenly.

'Sorry?' Sol was instantly on alert.

'Settling down with Anouk. Do you think you, the perennial playboy, can do that?'

'I'm not settling down,' Sol denied.

'Then why care? I mean, I get that you care about your patients, and the kids at the centre. But I've never known you to care about a woman enough to ask for my help.'

'She's...different.' He chose his words circumspectly. 'But that doesn't mean there's anything serious between us.'

'Right.'

Malachi pushed his chair back abruptly and stood up, moving to the window to look out, and it struck Sol that they were so alike, he and his brother.

Perhaps that was why, when he felt the disapproval radiating from Malachi's stiff back, Sol knew it wasn't actually directed at him. Rather, his brother was censuring himself. Which was why he took the plunge into the dangerous waters of asking personal questions.

'Who is she, Mal?'

Malachi swung around but said nothing. The silence seemed to arc between them, dangerous and electric, so many emotions charging over his brother's usually closed face that Sol could barely keep up. But he recognised anger, and he recognised fear.

What the hell could ever make his big, tough brother afraid?

'I think I prefer the Sol who just beds women and moves on,' Malachi said at length. 'You're acting like a lost puppy. Anouk's lost puppy, to be exact.'

But despite the way he bit out the words Sol knew his brother well enough to read that there was no malice behind them, and so he didn't take offence.

'Sod off.' He stood slowly and deliberately, then sauntered over to the sideboard and selected another pastry. A show of nonchalance. 'I'm no one's puppy.'

'Not usually, no.' Malachi shrugged. 'You're usually fending them off with a stick.'

'What? Puppies?' Sol quipped.

'Puppies, women, little old ladies.' Malachi folded his arms over his chest and shrugged. 'But I've never seen you look at anyone the way I saw you look at that one the night of the gala.'

'Her name's Anouk,' Sol corrected instinctively, before realising that Malachi was baiting him. His brother knew her name perfectly well. He'd already used it several times. 'And I didn't look at her any particularly special way.'

Malachi twitched one eyebrow upwards, but said nothing.

'No clever quip?' Sol demanded when he couldn't stand the heavy silence any longer.

'I told you, not this time.'

Sol sized up his big brother. There was something odd about Malachi, and it came back to the fact that the guy was more on edge than usual.

'What's going on, Mal?'

'Nothing.'

'You're being cagey.'

'Not really.' Mal dismissed it casually. Arguably a little too casually. 'No more so than you, anyway.'

'You're kidding, right?' Sol shook his head in disbelief.

'Not particularly.'

'Fine.' Leaning back on the sideboard, Sol eyed his brother. 'Time to tell me something I don't know, Mal. If you've got the balls for it.'

And just like that, they were two kids again, and Sol was pressing his brother on where he'd been that first time he'd done a job for the Mullen brothers.

Just as he began to think it wasn't going to work, Malachi opened his mouth.

'I always thought a wife, a family, wasn't for us. Not after everything with *her*.' Sol didn't answer; they both knew he meant their mother. 'I always thought I'd done that bit. I'd endured that responsibility. I never wanted to do it again.'

'But now?' Sol prompted.

'Lately... I don't know.' Malachi swung around from the window almost angrily. 'Forget it. I'm just... Forget I said anything.'

In all these years, they hadn't talked about what had happened. Or about feelings. They were the Gunn brothers. That wasn't the way they handled their issues. But suddenly, something was different. Not Anouk, of course.

He told himself that would be taking it too far. But...*something*. Maybe a delayed reaction to hitting his thirties. The incident with Izzy and her family. The responsibility of the centre.

'Are we capable of it, do you think, Mal?'

His brother frowned. 'Of what?'

'Of…love.'

'You love Anouk?'

'Don't be stupid,' Sol scoffed. 'I'm not saying that. It's just hypothetical.'

He hated himself for not sounding more convincing. It ought to—it was the truth after all. There was no way he could be *in love* with anyone. Let alone Anouk. Whatever they shared between the two of them, it wasn't love. Was it?

Sol waited for the harmless jeering but it didn't come. Instead, Malachi eyed him morosely.

'Hypothetically, I don't even know if we have that capacity,' Malachi gritted out unexpectedly. 'But maybe the question should be, do we deserve it?'

Sol didn't know how to answer, but it didn't matter because his brother was speaking again.

'More pertinently, does any woman deserve to be subjected to our love, *bratik*? Such as we know what that is.'

If his brother had punched him in the gut Sol

couldn't have felt any more winded. As if the air had been sucked from his very lungs.

Was Mal right? Would his love be more of a curse than any sort of a gift?

His mind was so full of conflicting thoughts that he simply let them jostle, his eyes scanning the room almost as a distraction. Which was when they alighted again on the Christmas tree.

'So, you and Saskia?'

'I don't wish to discuss it.' Malachi cut him off harshly.

'But you need to,' Sol answered. He rarely stood up to his brother, he rarely needed to. This, he felt, was different. This mattered. To both of them. 'Right here, right now. Our mother ruined both of our childhoods. It's time we both decided whether we're going to let her ruin our futures, too.'

'What have we got?' Sol asked, rounding the corner to the bay. It had been a hectic shift so far, but he thrived on that.

The young doctor running the case looked relieved.

'Darren, nineteen, he suffers from epilepsy and this morning he had two back-to-back seizures, which is out of the norm for him. Full tonic-clonic seizures usually months apart and often only if there's already something going on in the body, like an infection.'

'Has he got an infection?' Sol checked.

'I think an ear infection.'

'And you've started a course of antibiotics?'

'Yes.'

'So, possibly not neuro at this point. But keep me in the loop,' Sol confirmed. 'Okay, let me go and check in the next bay. I had a call for them, as well.'

He slipped around the curtain just as Anouk glanced up. Surprise swept over her face for a moment but she regrouped quickly.

'This is Jack, twenty-five. He was drinking and playing football in the park with a group of mates when he collided with a tree. Loss of consciousness for about five minutes. Pupils are unequal and reactive and he's agitated. We're taking him up to CT now.'

'I'll come with you,' Sol confirmed.

Unequal pupils suggested a bleed on the brain, which might be pushing against the brain itself.

'Great.' Anouk nodded, turning back to her team and issuing her final instructions. 'Let's go.'

'He isn't responding to us verbally, although he does react physically if we ask him to do something. I don't know if the verbal is about the alcohol or a possible injury.'

'Are you going to the centre tonight?' she asked quietly as they strode along the corridors behind the patient.

'Yes, why?'

'I was thinking of going.'

'Do you need a lift?' He frowned, not liking her caginess.

It felt like a huge step backwards, but he couldn't pinpoint why.

'No, I just thought that…maybe you'd prefer it if we weren't there together.'

'Why not?'

It shouldn't gnaw at him the way it did. He understood why she might think it should bother him.

'If that was going to be an issue then I wouldn't have invited you to visit in the first instance,' he told her.

Except he still didn't know what had motivated him to ask her. He refused to accept that it was some uncharacteristic need to have her see a different side to him. That didn't make sense.

Although it seemed the most logical conclusion.

'I just wasn't sure.' She lowered her voice even further as the team reached the CT department and people began to congregate. 'After our... one-night stand.'

Her sudden whisper almost made him laugh. Any other time it probably would have done. But Sol was too busy thinking how dismal the term sounded on Anouk's lips. It felt inadequate to describe either of their encounters that way.

One-night stand—admittedly lasting longer than just the one 'night' sounded, frankly, a little pitiful.

What was happening to him? Why was he reading so much into everything? They'd had a good time together. Twice. Surely he should be more than happy to accept it for what it was?

'I'm heading down there after work,' he informed her. 'I'll drive you, too.'

'Oh, it's okay, I can walk.'

'I'll come down to the department when I'm

done. If I'm caught up with a case, wait for me, we'll go together.'

It wasn't a request and they both knew it.

Still, when she flashed him a shy smile it twisted inside him, like a ribbon on a maypole. Delicate and pretty.

Sol snorted to himself as he stepped into the room. He was going to have to watch himself. If he wasn't careful then he risked Anouk wrapping herself around him in more ways than either of them could ever have anticipated.

CHAPTER TWELVE

THE CENTRE MIGHT as well have been Santa's grotto itself, Sol thought, surveying the scene in front of him—a hive of excitement and activity, it felt like the very epicentre of Christmas for the whole of Moorlands Wood.

And there, sitting on the floor, with Libby firmly wedged on one side of her and Katie on the other, pressing against her as though each claiming her as their own, was Anouk. It struck him that the girls' easy acceptance of her said more about Anouk than anything a person could say. These kids dealt with so much at such a young age that they often seemed to develop sixth senses about people.

This had to explain why he had let her slip under his skin without realising it. As he'd told Malachi, it wasn't anything as nonsensical as *love*.

Nevertheless, there was a draw there, a magnetism that pulled him in despite his vows to keep his distance. Which meant that, even now, he couldn't tear his gaze away.

Anouk looked totally engrossed in what she was doing. And what she was doing, he realised after a few moments' scrutiny, was measuring chocolate balls into a jar, before gluing reindeer antlers, funny eyes, and a big red nose onto the glass.

By the look of the full box in front of them, the trio had been working together for some time and were so focussed on the task in hand that none of them noticed him. And so he was free to stand and admire this fascinating woman who appeared, bizarrely, to have so captured his attention.

Without warning, Anouk looked up and her eyes—wide with surprise—locked with his. He didn't think, he didn't consider, he just reacted, flashing her a wide grin; something bursting inside him as she responded instinctively with a hint of a smile, her cheeks taking on a delicately pink hue.

Before he realised where he was, he had crossed the room and was standing in front of the trio. Still, it took him a supreme effort to tear his gaze from Anouk and greet the two young girls still nestled so lovingly on either side of her, as though seeking protection from her metaphorical wings.

'So we're making reindeer chocolate jars, are we?' he managed brightly.

'We've just finished.' Katie cast her arm over the full box solemnly. 'Now we're going to make beaded friendship bracelets for each other.'

'*Kruto!* Wow, they look amazing. Can I join in?' He felt Anouk's sharp gaze but he kept his eyes fixed on the girls, gratified when they nodded excitedly and got to their feet.

'We'll go and get the beads and the thread.' Libby grabbed Katie's arm. 'Why don't we use all green and red, like a Christmas theme?'

'Okay, but we should still have silver thread— that will make it brighter,' Katie advised as the two of them hurried off, lost in the carefree happiness of the moment and oblivious to the undertones that swirled around Sol and Anouk.

He settled himself on the floor next to her leaving a decent foot between them, but he still noticed her pulse leap at her throat as she deliberately avoided eye contact with him, inching another fraction away, as though she couldn't trust them to be so close to each other. It offered him a perverse kind of exultation.

At least he wasn't the only one feeling undercut by the intensity of the last week.

'Did you know this thing between Saskia and my brother is serious?'

He hadn't intended to say anything, but Malachi's revelations were still bubbling in his head and he couldn't help but wonder how much Anouk knew.

'Saskia and Malachi? No, how could I know?' Anouk frowned. 'I've been with you, and when I did return home she wasn't there.'

There was no reason for his body to tauten at the mere memory, surely?

'I hope he doesn't hurt her,' continued Anouk, obliviously. 'Saskia isn't as airy and tough as she might appear.'

'Funny, I was going to say the same thing about Malachi.'

She arched her eyebrows at him, waiting for some punchline. But he didn't have one. He was worried about his brother for the first time in for ever.

They weren't prepared for this...thing. Whatever it was. He might not have a name for it yet but he knew it was powerful. It assailed him at the most inopportune moments. Punching through him like a fist through wet paper. Like when he'd seen the naked sadness in her eyes when Anouk had told him about her father, or yesterday when he'd caught sight of her caring for her patient from across the ward, or today when she'd been so caught up with the girls that she hadn't even noticed anyone else in the room.

It wasn't love, but Sol imagined it was something in that family. He certainly *cared* for Anouk. So if whatever Mal felt for Saskia was anything like it, then he pitied his brother.

'Malachi won't hurt her. He isn't like me.'

The words came out automatically. Because he might once have believed them, although now he wasn't so sure.

'Because he isn't a playboy like you are, you mean?'

Why was it that it sounded so...hollow, coming off her tongue? Especially after the conversation they'd had in his apartment that night. It occurred to him that she might be testing him, but he had no idea how he was supposed to answer.

'You could say that,' he conceded, shocked at how much it cost him to sound so nonchalant.

'The Smoking Gun,' she added, and she didn't need to add a roll of her eyes. Her words spoke loud and clear all on their own. As if she was reminding herself of his reputation. Cautioning herself.

And it bothered him. Especially after their time together.

For years he had revelled in his reputation as a playboy, had been proud of the fact that he'd come out of his childhood with such a strong sense of self. He had never pretended to be something he wasn't. He loved being with women, but he had always hated the idea of a relationship with them—how much more honest could a man be?

Yet now, something had shifted and the names sounded toneless, even uncomfortable. Like a familiar old jacket that no longer suited—or fitted—him, but that he'd been trying to hold onto nonetheless.

His head was unusually hazy. As if some of its connections had been unexpectedly broken and it was trying to rewire itself using different paths.

He still wasn't quite sure what it meant.

'Great nickname, wasn't it?' he challenged,

but the words seemed to leave an unpleasant, metallic taste in his mouth.

This was absurd.

The...*thing* he felt for Anouk was absurd.

With her sweet smile and gentle demeanour she had succeeded in hooking him in a way he would not have believed possible a mere week ago. If he wasn't careful, she was the kind of woman who could easily tame him long enough to put him on a leash. But what had Malachi warned him? That a leopard didn't change its spots? That he was under some kind of spell now, but that when he came around again, all hell would break loose and the person he would most likely end up hurting would be Anouk herself?

And the idea of hurting her made him feel physically sick.

He needed to get up and move away. Now. Before it was too late.

Instead, he sat, perfectly still, not making even a sound. And still something swirled around them. He could feel it and he knew she could, too.

'We got loads of beads,' Libby's excited voice reached his ears from across the room.

Just one more night, he promised himself. Just one last time with Anouk, and then he'd find a way to end it without anyone getting hurt.

And when his eyes caught hers, widening a fraction, the pulse leaping at her throat, he knew she was thinking the same thing.

'Come home with me.' His voice was low and urgent, more a command than a request.

Anouk nodded, seconds before the girls raced back across the gallery floor to rejoin them, and he'd never wished for two hours to pass so expediently.

Last time they had barely got through the door before Sol had pulled her to him. This time, they barely made it to the lift.

Sol claimed her with such reverent kisses it was as though he was committing every detail of her touch to memory. Inscribing himself on her soul and she couldn't seem to get enough of him.

She could never seem to get enough. And that was the essential problem.

Even now, as he peeled off her clothing to kiss every last millimetre of her body, laying waste to her resolve and tearing down every last barrier between them, she couldn't do anything but let him.

A slave to him. Or a slave to her desire for him. Either way, it amounted to the same thing. He was making her forget their arrangement. He was making her want more.

And more again.

Worse, Anouk couldn't bring herself to care. So when he scooped her up to carry her through to the bedroom, muttering hoarsely about *not making it past the hallway otherwise*, all she could do was cling to him, pressing her body to his and meeting his possessive mouth with her own, greedy demands.

It was all she could do to ignore the tight emotions that tumbled through her when he laid her down so very reverently on the bed, removing the last of her clothes until she was naked before him, and rolling back to gaze at her, spread out before him as if she was his own personal feast.

'I've waited for this all day, *zolotse*,' he muttered, before lowering his mouth to her neck, kissing and licking the column of her throat, and fitting his palms to her breasts as if he couldn't bear not to touch her a moment longer.

He trailed scorching little kisses down her

neck and to the sensitive hollow at the base, taking his time, until she was urging him on with little moans. He moved across her shoulder and over the swell of her chest, inch by exquisite inch, as if he didn't want to skip over a single millimetre of her body until finally—*finally*—his mouth took over from his hands.

First he sucked one hard, aching nipple into his mouth, grazing his teeth over it gently but not too gently, flicking over it with his tongue, lavishing attention on her. And only when he seemed truly satisfied did he turn his attention to the other side, to repeat the same, adoring process.

And Anouk arched up to him as though to offer up more of herself, her whole body feeling heavy and restless and wanting more. So much more. But he held her in place, deliberately trapping her legs so she couldn't part them around him, couldn't draw him against her, couldn't nestle him where she burned for him most.

Like some kind of exquisite torture.

But if he didn't slide inside her soon, filling her up where all these wild sensations jousted in her, she didn't know if she could survive it.

Anouk didn't know when it occurred to her

that if he could torment her so wantonly, then surely she, too, could tease him?

Slowly, carefully, she ran her hands over his back, indulging, just for a moment or two, in reacquainting herself with those hewn muscles that not even his bespoke suit and waistcoat could conceal.

And when he murmured his approval, he answered her long and low, reverberating through her breasts and into her already molten core.

With deliberate care she slid one hand around his waist and wrapped her fingers delicately around his sex. The effect was instantaneous, making her feel womanly and powerful all at once.

'If you do that, you'll find this won't last anywhere as long as it could,' he growled, and she loved the rawness in his tone.

'That's the idea,' she whispered. 'Because I don't think I can hold out much longer.'

A primal sound slipped from his throat as he shifted from her, easing down her body and using his hand to move her legs apart.

'At last,' she sighed, waiting for him to settle between them.

But instead of his body, he edged down with

his shoulders, lifting his head only long enough for her to see the wicked gleam in his eyes.

'You can last,' he rasped. 'I insist on it.'

And then he buried his mouth, his tongue, into her heat, before she could answer, and she heard herself cry out.

Anouk had no idea how long he stayed there, paying homage to her as she could only clutch at his hair, his head, his shoulders, her raspy breath and abandoned cry the only sounds to break the silence. His murmurs of approval echoed through her, against her, as he feasted all the more making her shatter once, twice against his tongue then his fingers.

You are ruined, a voice whispered. *You will never, ever meet another man like Sol. There* is *no other man like Solomon Gunn.*

But she couldn't allow herself such thoughts. That path only led to misery. And so she ejected the unwelcome voice from her head and wriggled out from under Sol, pushing him onto his back, her eyes locking with his as she knelt over him and drew him deep into her mouth.

He was big and hot, like silky steel, and she forgot that she was meant to be distracting herself from the intimacy of his mouth on her body and instead lost herself in the intimacy of her tongue swirling over and around him. She was tormenting him and pleasuring him with every second. The way she'd learned to do this past week. The way she never seemed to tire of doing. She probably never would.

She shut the errant thought down once again, concentrating on the moment. Reminding herself that this was just about sex. Only ever about sex.

There could be nothing more.

Lifting her eyes, she made herself focus on Sol. The intensity of his gaze and the unmistakeable shudder of need that took over his body made her feel powerful, and wicked. And all woman. She sucked him in deeper, wanting to lose herself inside that power, in a way she'd never enjoyed with any man before Sol.

Only Sol.

But apparently he wasn't prepared to let things end on her terms. With a low, primal groan, he pulled himself from her mouth and flipped her onto her back as he moved his body to cover hers. His hands traced every inch of her as though she was a revelation to him. It was incredible how precious, how *special*, she always felt when she was in his arms. Yet she was too hot, too needy, for any more play.

As though reading her mind, Sol shifted, nestling between her legs until she could feel his blunt end dipping into her.

'Please, Sol,' she breathed, desperate to lose herself in the primitive sensations that might drown out the other, more dangerous emotions that tumbled in her chest.

Emotions she told herself she had no name for.

Even as she was altogether too afraid that she could name them. Every last one.

And when Sol finally thrust inside her, deep and slow and sure, his gaze holding hers, she refused to let her eyes slide from him. She held her breath, for fear the words she refused to face might fall from them.

Sol moved, pulling out of her before driving home again. Deeper, tighter, hungrier. Driving her faster and faster towards the top. When she finally catapulted over the edge, and heard herself cry out his name, his eyes still holding hers as he followed her, she knew the truth in her heart but she still wasn't prepared to hear Sol say it out loud.

Clear and raw, as though the words had been ripped from the very depths of his soul.

'I love you, *zolotse*.'

'No,' she choked out. Then, louder, *'No!'*

'I'm in love with you, Anouk.' He tried the words again, rolling them around on his tongue, still in shock.

He was in shock. He hadn't intended to say them, much less repeat them, and yet the inexplicable thing was that the more he said them out loud, the easier it felt. The more he liked the way they tasted in his mouth, the way they sounded to his ears.

Like a melody he'd thought he would never want to hear.

'You can't say that.' She was furious. 'I won't hear it. Take it back.'

'Not possible,' he managed. 'It's out there and it can't be taken back.'

She stared at him as though he had physically wounded her.

'Why are you doing this?'

Her evident confusion clawed at his heart. It wasn't as if he understood completely himself. And yet, each time he said it, it made more sense.

Everything made more sense.

'I swore I would never fall in love with any woman. Ever. But here I am. And I know you feel the same way about me.'

'I don't,' she choked, scrambling to get off him. *Away* from him.

He let her, even as he emitted a laugh at the irony of it.

He, who had spent over a decade steering clear of relationships with women who would inevitably declare themselves in love with him, was now in love.

It seemed only fitting that *he* should be the one saying it whilst the woman he loved didn't want to accept it. As if it was a test of his own making. He'd never failed a damned test in his entire career, he wasn't about to start now.

'Our deal was sex. Pure and simple,' she cried, spinning around searching for her clothes. 'You're the king of one-night stands.'

'I was. Until you came along.'

He watched her locate her T-shirt and pull it on, then flail around for her jeans. He didn't try to stop her, he didn't want her to feel trapped or cornered, but he didn't share her fluster. He just felt calm. At peace.

It was odd, the way the minute he'd admitted that he loved her, everything had seemed to start slotting into place, piece by piece. He felt somehow...*whole.*

'You said it yourself—I used sex as a distraction.' He shrugged. 'That I just needed to meet the right person. Turns out you were right.'

'No. No, I wasn't.' She shoved her feet into her jeans, first one and then the other, before yanking them up those slender legs that had spent so much of the night wrapped around him. 'You told me that I didn't know the first thing about you. That I was reading too much into it because I wanted you to be a better man than you really are.'

'Turns out I was wrong.'

'No!' Her voice sounded mangled, wretched, and his heart actually ached for her.

'You can deny it as many times as you like, Anouk. It won't change it, believe me. I've been pretending to myself that there was nothing more than sex between us—just like you are now—but I can't pretend any longer.'

'Then try,' she half choked, half bit out.

She looked wounded, and fragile, and even more beautiful than ever. As if finally acknowledging the truth had infused his whole world with a more vivid colour.

How had he ever thought that love was destructive? How had he failed to realise just how glorious it could be?

'More to the point,' he told her quietly, 'I don't want to pretend that it's just sex any more.'

'This is about the chase. You only think you love me because I'm the first woman who made you work for it. Because you had to give a little of yourself, telling me about your childhood and your hardships, in order to get closer to me.'

'You're wrong, Anouk.' At one time her words would have got under his skin, clawing at him, leaving scars. All he felt now was calm acceptance. It was enough to steal his breath away.

'You've confused lust for love.'

'I've never confused lust for anything.' He smiled. 'I always welcomed it, indulged in it. I don't love you because you are the first woman who made me work for you. I love you because you're the only woman who has ever made me *want* to work for it.'

'I don't want this.' She shook her head, sounding as if she was trying to swallow a sob. 'You can't do this to me.'

He stood with deliberate care, so as not to startle her. And despite all her protestations she froze, her eyes fixed on his body, the naked longing in them belying every word she was trying to tell him.

'I think you *do* want this, Anouk.' He reached for his own jeans, pulling them on slowly. Controlled. 'And I think that's what you're most afraid of. That, and the fact that it means trusting another person for the first time in your life.'

'I trust Saskia,' she shot back.

'This is different. *Love* is different. We both know that.'

'I can't offer you that.' Stumbling to the door, she gripped the handle so tightly that her knuckles went white. 'I can't offer you anything. I don't have the capacity for it.'

'Did I ask for anything? I told you I love you; I never demanded that you say it back. But, for what it's worth, you *do* have the capacity for it and one day you will realise it. Trust me. But until that day comes, I have enough love for both of us.'

He watched her stop, sucking in one deep breath after another and straightening her shoulders.

When she turned to him, he could see the forged steel in her eyes. But, behind the steel, stuffed as far back as she could manage, he could also see a desperate yearning to believe.

'You don't know what love is, Sol. Any more than I do. You don't care. Right now, it's thrilling because I've made you feel something you've never felt before. But whatever it is, it isn't love.'

'It's love, Anouk,' he assured her, calmly and quietly, because he'd never been so sure of anything in his life. 'I thought I wasn't capable of it. It turns out I just wasn't capable of it with anybody but you.'

'They're just hollow words,' she gasped, and even as she tried to argue he knew she was struggling to stay standing. 'I know that even if you don't, which is why I'm leaving now. And one day, in the not too distant future, no doubt, you'll thank me for it.'

'I want you to do whatever it is that you need to do, Anouk. I won't thank you for leaving, but neither will I blame you for it. Just as long as you remember you can come back.'

'You're so sure of yourself, aren't you? So arrogant.' She blinked, apparently not realising she'd raised her voice until she heard it echoing back at her.

'I've never apologised for who I am.' He kept his voice even. 'So yes, I'm willing to bet on myself. You'll come back to me. It's inevitable.'

'I'll never come back,' she gritted out.

Then she opened the door and lurched out, leaving him where he stood.

Sol had no idea how long he stood there, not moving, barely even daring to breathe. Waiting for Anouk to walk back through the doorway.

But she didn't. The truth was that he didn't know if she ever would. Yet he regretted nothing. He loved her.

He had never loved any other woman. He knew he never would.

All he could do was hope that she was as strong as he thought she was. That she would be able to trust herself and admit what he already knew to be true.

Anouk loved him, too.

And he could hope that, one day, he would have the chance to *prove* to her that he cared. That his actions would tell her he loved her in a way that she could believe, even if she couldn't accept his words.

Maybe it would take days, perhaps weeks. It could even take years. But he had to believe it would happen.

And when it did, he wouldn't miss his chance.

CHAPTER THIRTEEN

'THIS IS ADAM. He's eight years old and he fell approximately eight feet over the retaining wall at the bottom of his garden and onto grass below. He is normally fit and well with no allergies. He's not on any meds and he's up to date with all his jabs. He was playing at the bottom of the garden with his sister when the fence gave way and he fell down to the grass below, landing on his face and knocking out two teeth and there are a couple more loose in his mouth. He suffered a loss of consciousness of approximately one minute. Mum travelled in the helicopter with us, and Dad is on his way by car.'

'You have the teeth?'

'In some milk in there.' The HEMS doctor indicated a plastic fruit box his colleague was carrying.

'Okay, thank you.' Anouk bobbed her head. 'Okay, guys, let's get started.'

As her colleagues worked to set up the drips

and take the bloods for testing, Anouk concentrated on the young boy.

'Adam? Can you hear me, sweetie? My name is Anouk and I'm the doctor who will be making you better. Can you tell me what happened, at all?' She turned to her team. 'Let's give him two point five mil of morphine, try to make him more comfortable.'

'Sure.' Her colleague nodded. 'Do you want me to get Maxillofacial?'

'Good idea,' she agreed. 'Give them a shout. Okay, let's get this little boy comfortable so that we can get him for a CT scan and check what's going on in his head.'

Even as she spoke, the monitors began to bleep, and her colleagues around the boy simultaneously declared the patient was becoming breathless.

'He's going tachycardic,' Anouk warned. 'Let's bag him.'

'Do you want to intubate?'

Anouk frowned. Adam's airway was at risk because if one of those loose teeth dislodged and he inhaled it, it could potentially block off his airway.

'He hasn't stopped breathing,' she confirmed.

'Let's see if we can't give OMS a chance to see him first.'

And the sooner she could get the little boy to the scanner to check his brain, the better.

'You've been avoiding me.'

Anouk jumped at the quiet voice by her shoulder. She didn't look up from the screen but she could no longer see a single word or image that was now swimming in front of her eyes.

'No,' she tried to deny it. 'I've just been… busy.'

It was partially true. She had been busy. Mostly she'd been busy trying not to relive his declaration to her, because she honestly didn't know how she felt about it.

She was supposed to not believe in love. She had spent years telling herself what love looked like and it had been an ugly, selfish, cruel image that she'd painted in her own head.

But the minute those very same words had come out of Sol's mouth, they had erased all of it, leaving something so beautiful, and precious, almost ethereal in their stead. Almost too perfect to be real.

So how could she trust it?

'I don't regret saying it,' he announced softly, as though he could read her thoughts.

The worst thing about it was that she so wanted to believe him.

'I'm sorry... I can't.' She shook her head, her words almost lost between her voice box and her ears. 'They're just words. They don't prove anything.'

'You need to come with me.'

'I'm working.'

'The place is quiet. In an hour it probably won't be, but, for now, you have half an hour. Come with me.'

She didn't need to hear him move to sense that he was leaving without her. She ought to let him.

Rising from her stool, with just another quick glance around to check that all was okay, Anouk followed him out of Resus.

'Where are we going?'

The winding nature of the old part of the hospital seemed to conspire with Sol to add to the sense of suspense today.

It had been a good day. Even her young patient, Adam, had defied the odds to avoid any serious injuries.

'You'll see.' Sol didn't slow his pace.

She tried not to dwell on the fact that he sounded so serious and intent. It was just her second-guessing herself. Not wanting to give away the fact that she'd realised she was doing something as wholly and utterly stupid as falling for the man.

She'd have to be an idiot to forget who she was dealing with.

And the worst thing about it was that she seemed to be exactly that idiot.

Where *was* Sol leading?

'We're going to the cafeteria?' she guessed, as she stretched out her stride trying to keep up with him.

He seemed sharper, edgier than usual.

'Yes.'

'Sol, it's been a long shift. I don't want to eat here. I'd rather just finish my shift and go home.'

'You're not eating here.' He stopped, taking her chin in his hands and tilting her head up to his.

The look he shot her was altogether too hot, and she shivered at the naughty thoughts that he could stir up with just a glance.

Her breath caught in her chest. Almost painful as it lodged there.

'What's going on, Sol?'

He turned her so that she was looking in through the internal cafeteria window.

'Can you see that woman sitting at the table over there? Sixties to seventies? Red coat on the back of the chair?'

Anouk scanned the room, focussing on the area where he was pointing. There was no reason in the world for her heart to thump. But it did.

'Why? Who is she?'

'That's your grandmother, Anouk. Your father's mother. Mal found her.'

Something dark, and angry, and...*panicky* rolled through her.

'Malachi did?' She could hear things crashing around her. It took a moment to realise it was in her head. 'You had your brother *track her down*?'

How could Sol have contacted her grandmother behind her back? How could he have brought her here? How could he have ambushed her like this?

Anouk didn't know how long she stood there. Probably only a few seconds but it felt like days. Her hands were clenched so tightly that her fingernails scored marks deep into her palms. And then she was spinning around, plunging back across the room, knocking chairs flying outside a consultation room, but wholly unable to stop, or turn, or pick them back up.

Sol caught up with her as she tore along the corridor away from the dining area.

'Anouk, stop. *Stop.* Don't run away.'

'Don't run away?' she snapped, her voice just about managing to work again. 'Don't *run away*?'

This time it was louder. She felt Sol's hands on her shoulders and she shrugged them off with a violence she would never have thought she possessed.

'Anouk—'

'How *dare* you do that to me?' she roared, because it was either that or give into this thing spiralling inside her that would make her crumple and fold.

She was dimly aware of Sol checking up and down the corridor as staff moved curiously through, before he tested a few doors and then pulled her into a consultation room. She didn't know whose. She didn't care.

Fear and anger duelled inside her, and she couldn't risk letting the former win.

'You just need to hear her out, Anouk.' Even the black look on his face couldn't deter her.

'Why, because *you* think I should? I'm not ready to do that yet. And you don't get to be the one to order me otherwise.'

'I'm trying to help you,' he growled.

The worst of it was that a part of her believed him. She barked out a hollow, unpleasant laugh, all the better to drown out the pounding of her blood through her veins.

'By dictating to me? My, how lucky am I?'

'You're twisting what's happening here.' Sol reached out as though he was going to take hold of her shoulders again, then thought better of it and rammed his hands in his pockets.

Half of her gave herself a satisfied air-punch whilst the other half lamented the loss. She felt twisted inside out, as if she didn't know who or where she was. Everything was wrong. Unsettled.

'And here, of all places?'

'It's neutral territory. You're a skilled doctor. This is where you feel safe and confident. It will translate into the conversation.'

'No, it won't,' she gritted out. 'Because there isn't going to be a conversation.'

'Anouk, don't be scared…'

'I'm not scared,' she cried, the lie mocking her even as it hung in the air. 'I'm an idiot but I'm not scared.'

'You are and you're lashing out. And that's fine. But you don't need to be frightened. I'm here to support you.'

'Support me? You?' She laughed, a brittle, harsh sound. 'You can't support me, or anyone. I was wrong when I said that you knew how to care for someone, how to love them. You don't have it in you to think of anyone but yourself. Deciding you know what's best for me without thinking to discuss it with me for one single second. My God, you even said the words to me. But you don't know what they mean. You don't know what it is to love someone. You're every bit as selfish and arrogant as you said you were.'

And before she could fall apart completely in front of him, Anouk whirled herself around and ran—as fast as she possibly could.

Sol watched her go, her words stinging him as if every one had been a knife going into his heart.

He'd hoped that bringing her here would resolve the impasse between them. He'd hoped it would show her that he was sincere. That he wanted to be worthy of her.

He loved her.

It had been almost a week since he'd told her. Since he'd heard himself say the words out loud. And oddly, it was getting easier and easier to accept, with each passing day. He'd always thought love was something to fear but Anouk made it seem like something special. Something new. Something to *aspire* to, rather than dread.

Unlike any other woman he had dated, he knew, he just knew, that Anouk understood why he had to be a part of centres like Care to Play. She would never pout, or complain, or moan that the kids got more of his time than she did. Or that she would rather be going to a fancy, high-society gala than another football-and-barbecue-in-the-park event. In fact, Anouk would most likely be right there beside him. Organising every single event.

She made everything shift and change when she was around. People, places, situations. They all sparkled that little brighter under her touch. And Sol wanted, more desperately than he could remember wanting anything for such a long time, to be a part of her life.

It made no sense, yet here he was fighting every instinct to go after her and *make* her listen to him.

He had to let her go—for now. The best thing he could do would be to take a leaf out of the book of the woman sitting in that cafeteria back there. The woman who was so utterly desperate to meet her granddaughter for the first time, and who had longed for this moment for over three decades yet still had the patience to wait that little bit longer.

Turning around, Sol strode back down the corridor. For one thing, he owed the older woman an apology and, for a second, she was the closest thing to a source he had on Anouk.

He could give Anouk her space, but still, the more he understood this complex and enigmatic woman who had somehow crept inside the heart he'd thought locked down for good, the better.

At least he knew one thing. Tracking down Anouk's grandmother had been the right thing to do. Whether Anouk wanted to accept the truth or not, it was clear that she needed to meet her other grandmother and learn what had really happened between her father and her mother.

Until Anouk had closure, for better or for worse, she was never going to be able to move past it and into a relationship with anyone.

With *him*.

Anouk had no idea how long she stood at the bright green front door, her eyes locked balefully onto the Christmas wreath and her hand poised to knock but her heart clattering much too wildly against her ribs to let her. So when the door opened, almost cautiously, she almost stumbled back down the steps.

'Hello, Anouk.'

It took a moment for Anouk to realise that she was still standing with her arm raised. She lowered it—it felt like in slow motion—but still couldn't work her mouth enough to answer.

'You've been standing there for the better part of ten minutes. Would you like to come in?'

Would she? Her mind felt split in two.

Stiffly, she bobbed her head, trying not to allow the older woman's soft smile to work its way inside her, and let herself be ushered carefully into the house.

A string of Christmas cards adorned the hallway, testament to how popular this new grandmother of hers appeared to be, and a decent, prettily decorated tree stood proudly in one corner of the living room.

'Your father decorated it every year. For me,' she was told by this older woman whom Anouk supposed was her grandmother. 'I don't think he ever had one at his own home. He always said Christmas was for the children, and he'd enjoy it when he had you to share it with.'

Anouk didn't know how to respond.

A couple of minutes later they were sitting in silence at a small, glossy, yew dining table with quaint coasters in front of them and a teapot, cups and saucers, and a quintessential plate of biscuits. It was so utterly English that Anouk had to swallow a faintly hysterical gurgle.

'I got the bag,' she managed awkwardly after what felt like an age. Maybe two.

Someone—presumably Sol—had left it in Resus for her the next day. But he hadn't been to see her.

She told herself it was for the best.

Her companion nodded and offered an encouraging smile. It occurred to Anouk that the older woman—it was hard to think of her as her paternal grandmother—was as nervous as she was, if not more so.

Somehow, the knowledge bolstered her.

'It meant a lot. I never…knew…'

'There are more bags like that,' her grandmother said sadly. 'Full up. Every Christmas, every birthday, without fail. We gave up sending them to you—they always got returned. But we never gave up on you.'

'I didn't even know you wrote to me,' she managed, her voice thick. 'I only knew about one letter, but I didn't know what it said, or when it had been sent.'

'We wrote to you all the time. Letters at first, as you saw in that bag. But diaries after a while.'

'Oh.' Anouk took a sip of tea by way of distracting herself, but suddenly it was impossible to swallow.

'Do you want to see them?'

Her grandmother pushed her chair back and Anouk almost fell over herself to stop her.

'*No.*' She hadn't meant to make the older woman jump. 'No. Sorry. It's just…'

'Too much to take at once,' her grandmother guessed. 'Another time, perhaps.'

'Another time,' Anouk agreed, surprised to realise that she really meant it.

She still hadn't processed the emotions that had crashed over her, threatening to overwhelm her, when she'd looked into that bag and found a selection of gifts from when she was a baby, to this very year.

The letters that had accompanied them— the first few marked *Return to Sender* in her mother's unmistakeable loopy handwriting— had been like a sledgehammer to her heart. Every word thumping painfully into her. Words she'd longed to hear as a kid but which her self-obsessed mother had never once uttered to her.

Her father and her grandmother had each penned letters that had been so heartfelt, so pained, that Anouk couldn't have denied their veracity even if she'd wanted to. Which she didn't.

They spoke about how much they loved her, how the dimples on her baby cheeks, or the gurgle of her laugh, had filled them with such pride, such joy, and such a feeling of completeness. And the only thing that had undercut it all had been the fact that the two of them had been compelled to snatch every snippet they could from the magazine articles, or the news items, or the TV interviews, in which her mother had trotted her out with the sole reason of making herself look like a good and doting mother.

It had taken Anouk almost two days to track down a VHS player so that she could see the recordings her father had made on the two occasions he'd travelled to the States to try to speak to Annalise Hartwood, only for her security team to practically manhandle him away.

So much for her mother's claims that her father had wanted nothing to do with them.

'He wanted to be with you from the moment he knew Annalise was pregnant.' Her grandmother shook her head when Anouk voiced her thoughts out loud. 'He even proposed.'

'My father proposed?' Anouk felt her stomach twist. All the stories her mother had told her seemed more and more like lies. The worst of it was that she knew, instantly, that the version of events this relative stranger was recounting made more sense than anything Annalise had ever said.

'But your mother didn't want to know. She was rich and famous and he was nobody. Even when you came along there was nothing he could do.

She refused to acknowledge him as the father, let alone allow him to have contact. But he did try, you must know that.'

'I do now,' Anouk murmured.

At least Annalise had never tried to pretend her father was someone else. The one consolation she had was that the identity of her father had remained constant throughout the years, even if only to her.

'He was so proud of the way you were growing up. He would have been over the moon to know you'd become a doctor. And that you'd come over to the UK.'

'I wish I had tried to make contact sooner. I just... I always thought... I was led to believe...'

'That he didn't want to know you,' her grandmother supplied.

Incredibly there was no bitterness or rancour to the older woman's tone, just a deep kind of grief, even as they both silently knew that Annalise had been the one to pour all that poison.

'It couldn't have been further from the truth.' Her eyes shimmered and Anouk ducked her head for a moment, pretending she didn't notice.

She didn't want to succumb, as well. There seemed little point in telling the woman—her grandmother—that she'd gone to his house years ago. That could be a discussion for another time.

'You have a good one there, you know.'

'A good one?' Anouk frowned as her grandmother smiled warmly.

'Solomon. The young man you're courting… or I should say dating, shouldn't I?'

'Oh. No. We're just friends.' She could feel the blush creeping up her neck and she knew her grandmother's surprisingly sharp eyes hadn't missed it.

Even the older woman's smile was suddenly faintly delighted.

'You don't go to the lengths your young man went to, or talk about a young lady the way he talked about you, if you're just friends. Take my word for it.'

'You're wrong.' Anouk flushed, but she could feel the tiny smile playing at the corners of her mouth, the spearhead of hope working its way around her heart like a sharp screwdriver prying the lid off an old tin of paint.

For the rest of the conversation, Anouk listened as her grandmother recounted some stories about her father, revelling in their obviously close relationship and trying not to resent her mother for keeping her from such a loving home.

She learned how her father had never married, his heart always belonging to her mother and herself, as cruelly as Annalise had treated him. Anouk didn't know if that made him single-minded or, frankly, a bit of a wet lettuce, but she liked to think of him as loyal and loving. And for now, that would work.

Her grandmother had an unexpectedly naughty sense of humour, which began to shine through once their initial nervousness had been overcome. And, Anouk discovered to her shock, the older woman had been very happily married three times. Widowed all three times.

'I was a bit of a saucy young lady,' her grandmother told her, 'but I loved each one of them very dearly. And I was always a good and faithful wife.'

And then the older woman twinkled in a way that Anouk suddenly realised was all too familiar. She had caught a glimpse of it in herself every now and then over the years, usually when Saskia had convinced her to relax on those rare nights out, but especially recently when Sol had been a part of her life.

Was it possible that Sol, like this woman with the twinkling eyes, had been a *bit saucy* until he'd found his soul mate? Could it be that she was Sol's? That Sol really did love her?

Anouk filed that little nugget in a box to dissect later. When she was alone. When she had the courage.

Still, the afternoon was emotionally exhausting. No doubt even more so for her grandmother.

'Maybe I should go,' Anouk hazarded after a while. 'I think I need to…absorb some of this.'

Her grandmother's eyes raked over her. The evident need for time to regroup obviously warring with the fear of never seeing her new granddaughter again.

'I'll come back,' Anouk added quickly. 'If you're happy for that, of course.'

A slender hand covered hers instantly, its grasp surprisingly strong.

'Do you promise me?'

It was so small a gesture, yet so strong, making something kick hard in her chest.

'I do,' she choked out.

'And you'll thank that young man of yours?'

Despite herself, Anouk couldn't help but smile.

'I told you, he isn't my young man.'

'He is if you want him to be,' came the surprising response.

For a moment, Anouk turned the idea over in her head.

Was he?

She wrinkled her nose and tried not to reveal her emotions. Everything seemed to be running so close to the surface these days, it was so unlike her usual self.

'No. I don't know if it really was once the case,' she heard herself confessing. 'But, if it was, it isn't any more.'

'That's up to you, my flower. I know enough about men to know that one is yours for the taking. If you want him, go and get him.'

Anouk wasn't sure if it was the grandmotherly advice or the term of endearment that tugged at her the most, but all of a sudden she had to fight the urge to break down. Right there and then.

But on the way home, her mind couldn't stop spinning. The events of the past hour, and the past few weeks, all whirling around her head. She was a mess.

She was never a mess.

But was it because of her father? Her grandmother? Or just Sol? And, more significantly, how was she going to sort it—and herself—out? Whatever this thing was inside her, this gnawing, empty, hollow thing, it needed Sol to assuage it. She wasn't prepared to go back to the life she'd had before him. She needed him. And whatever the hell that meant—they would work it out together.

If Sol really was hers for the taking, how on earth was she to even set about doing such a thing?

And then it came to her. What had Libby once said about Christmas Eve being the most magical time? First, she was going to need to take a detour to the Care to Play centre.

CHAPTER FOURTEEN

SOMETHING WAS DIFFERENT.

His home was...*changed.*

He had spent the entire day looking for Anouk. Checking her apartment, the hospital, the centre, even phoning Saskia so many times that an irritated Malachi had told him to give it up and go home for the night.

He hadn't wanted to.

The moment he'd heard that Anouk had approached Malachi for her grandmother's address, the need to find Anouk and ensure that she was okay had been overwhelming. He had no idea what her grandmother had ultimately told her and the fear that she was somewhere, alone and hurting, tore him up in a way he would never have believed possible.

If she was traumatised, then it would be his fault. He'd never intended for her to be ambushed by the knowledge of a grandmother she'd never met. He'd expected to be with her when they first met. And now he couldn't find Anouk anywhere. She had to be somewhere.

All he could do was head home and try again tomorrow. She couldn't hide out from him for ever. He wouldn't let her. He couldn't.

Sol stood, the front door still open behind him, as he tried to work out what it was. Slowly, as if his mind couldn't believe what his body already sensed, he kicked the door to and moved carefully to the archway.

The scene beyond was like something out of his childhood.

The main lights were low, and the place was illuminated with pretty, twinkling Christmas lights whilst a miniature winter, Christmas village covered the entire room, from little shops and houses to ice-skating rinks, Ferris wheels and small-gauge trains.

Beyond it all, Anouk stood, her hands twisted together and her face set in an anxious expression.

'What *is* this?' he demanded, his voice thick through his constricted throat.

He told himself not to believe, not to hope. He needed to wait, and hear the words.

'An apology.' Her voice was ragged, no better than his, and he allowed himself a moment to take that in.

To some degree it made him feel better. Still, he jammed his fists into his pockets as if that might stop him from striding across the room and reaching out for her the way he wanted to.

He moved further inside, wanting to kiss her. Claim her.

But by the way her arms were in front of her chest, her fingers knotting together, he had a feeling she needed to explain herself. Though perhaps not before babbling nervously a little first.

He could let her have that, too. After all, he wasn't entirely sure he knew what to say, himself.

'I went to see my grandmother today,' she breathed, a note of awe in her voice. 'She told me that I had to thank you.'

'I shouldn't have ambushed you at the hospital that day.' He exhaled sharply. 'I just thought that maybe the location would be the best place for you to feel in control. Strong.'

'It's okay.' She jerked forward, as though she was going to step up to him, before stopping awkwardly. 'I owe you an apology, for all those awful things I said. They were horrible, unkind. I'm so, so sorry.'

'Forget about them.' Closing the gap he caught her hands, trying to make her look at him. If she did, then he might be able to convince her that it really didn't matter.

She'd been frightened and cornered and she'd lashed out. Hell, he knew that feeling only too well.

'I can't. I didn't mean them…'

'I know. Anouk, look at me.' He crooked his finger under her chin. 'Forget it. Really.'

'I can hardly believe you did that for me.' Anouk smiled wanly, and, to Sol, even that was like the sunshine cracking through the heaviest sky after a thunderstorm. 'I can hardly believe you *cared* enough to do it.'

'It wasn't a big deal.'

'It was to me,' she said earnestly. 'No one has ever bothered to do anything like that for me before. Not unless they thought they could get something out of it. Usually access to my mother.'

'She did quite a number on you, didn't she?' Sol frowned as Anouk pulled away from him abruptly.

'My mother was...manipulative,' she confessed unexpectedly, her frankness taking him by surprise. 'She treated me like a precious daughter in public, but in private I was an inconvenient burden she couldn't stand to look at. And I was so desperate for her affection that I spent my whole life, whilst she was alive, turning myself inside out trying to win it. I even made myself sick trying to do everything I could for her. For her love.'

'The fault was never yours,' Sol said, shoving his clenched fists into his pockets just so that he wouldn't haul her into his arms.

He mustn't crowd her. She would come to him fully when she was ready.

'I know that. Logically.' She pulled a wry face. 'But I grew up in Hollywood, where there are altogether too many sycophants willing to excuse my mother's behaviour and agree that she was a saint and I was a problem child. And I was too young, too needy, too naïve to argue.'

'So you ended up believing them?'

'I saw a twisted kind of relationship where people used each other, all the while bandying about the word *love*. So I learned it can be a flawed, cruel concept more effective as a weapon than any kind of gift.'

Anger barrelled through him that someone as sweet, intelligent, and kind as Anouk could have allowed people who were *nothing* to drag her down and think less of herself. She seemed so strong, so sure, it was hard to believe it was just an act.

And yet…not hard at all. Because he saw her. Her virtues and her flaws. And he loved her despite them, or maybe *for* them.

'I know you don't believe me when I tell you that I love you, but it's true, Anouk. I love you with every fibre of who I am and, if you'll let me, I'll spend the rest of our lives trying to make you believe that.'

It felt like an eternity that she stood, watching him, immobile. And then suddenly she took his hand in her smaller ones.

'That's the point, Sol.' She smiled. 'I already believe you.'

It was like a thousand victories all spiralling through him at once.

'What changed?' He couldn't help but ask.

'You, contacting my grandmother. It showed

you listened to me, you cared, and you understood.'

'I'll always listen to you, Anouk.'

'I think I really believe that,' she agreed. 'It's why I came back, and why I did this,'

He followed her head as it scanned the room, encompassing the entire Christmas scene, not realising that he was pulling her back, closer to him, as he did so.

And, what was more, she was letting him.

'I love it,' he murmured, not entirely sure which bit he was talking about.

'It was the one thing I could think of to show you I had listened, too,' Anouk babbled. 'Even if you and Malachi aren't into it any more, except for the kids.'

'Shh. I love that you wanted to do something for me. I love that you thought about this, especially when I know how much you hate Christmas. It makes it all the more special that you did this for me.'

'It wasn't as bad as I'd feared,' she admitted.

'That's good.'

'It is?'

'Sure.' He grinned suddenly. 'It bodes well for any kids we might have.'

'You want children with me?' Anouk breathed in wonder.

'If you'd like that.' He slid his fingers to her chin, tilting her head up until they were eye to eye.

Deep down, she'd always wondered if she would ever want to be a mother. She'd doubted she had it in her. Her life had been about her career as a doctor and nothing else had ever pulled at her.

And then Sol had slammed into her life and everything had changed. She might not have considered babies with him before, but the moment he had mentioned it there had been no doubt in Anouk's mind that she wanted nothing more than to start a life—and a family—with him.

'I want children with you,' she managed, then seemed to draw in a deep breath. 'And, as for Christmas, it turns out my father always wanted to celebrate the holiday with me. He might not be here, but maybe I can do it in memory of him? Maybe you can help me?'

He felt his mouth crook, a sense of triumph punching its way through him. Who would have thought it would feel this good to be wanted by a woman like Anouk? To want her back?

Before he could answer, she was speaking again. Suddenly serious. 'And you were right, of course. I was running away.'

'Understandable,' he growled. 'Given the circumstances.'

She shook her head.

'You misunderstand me.' She ran her tongue over her teeth, her nerves clearly threatening to get the better of her in a way that touched him deeply. 'I wasn't just running away from my grandmother. Or my fear that whatever she or my late father had to say, it wouldn't match up to the fantasy in my head. I was also running away from you. Or, more to the point, my growing feelings for you.'

It was more than he'd thought she would say. More than he could have hoped she would say. He couldn't bite his tongue any longer.

'Whatever you were worried about, don't be. I love you, Anouk Hart, with all that I am.'

It was the look of wonder in her eyes that made his heart swell so wildly that he feared his chest couldn't contain it.

'You still love me?' she whispered, her eyes scanning his, almost in disbelief.

'I will *always* love you. You had to know that,

otherwise why come here?' He arced his arm around the room. 'Why do all of this?'

'Because *I* love *you*, you idiot.' She snorted, half laughing, half sobbing.

The words spun around him, lifting him and making him feel somehow complete.

'I can't believe you did all this yourself,' he told her at length when the breath in his chest finally felt like his again.

'Not all myself.' Anouk offered a wry smile. 'I had a little help. Quite a bit, in fact.'

'Is that so?'

'Libby, Katie and Isobel.'

He groaned loudly, but only half-heartedly.

'You realise those girls will for ever be able to say that I was wrong and they were right?'

'I do.' Her eyes twinkled mischievously, sending a streak of desire straight through him. 'Just as I know you won't begrudge them a moment of it.'

'I won't,' he murmured, revelling in the way Anouk's body was finally moulding to him.

As if she'd always been meant to be there.

'I love you,' he repeated, just because it felt incredible to say it. Because he couldn't get enough of hearing it. Because he didn't think he'd ever tire of basking in the tender glow of her sapphire gaze when he told her how he felt about her.

Now that her barriers had finally dropped.

'I love you, too, Solomon Gunn,' she whispered fiercely, all her tentativeness put aside in that moment. 'And I will continue loving you for the rest of my life.'

'I intend to hold you to that,' he managed gruffly, 'because I think it will take a lifetime to prove to you how much I love you, too.'

'Just the one?' she teased.

'Trust me, that's all we'll need, you and I. Together.'

He couldn't hold back a moment longer. Lowering his head, he claimed her mouth with his, letting her wind her arms around his neck, and lifting her up so that she could wrap her legs around his hips, as her heat poured through him.

And then he laid her down within their twinkling, magical Christmas village scene, and they welcomed in the first perfect Christmas of the rest of their lives together.

* * * * *

LET'S TALK
Romance

For exclusive extracts, competitions
and special offers, find us online:

f facebook.com/millsandboon

⊙ @millsandboonuk

🐦 @millsandboon

Or get in touch on 0844 844 1351*

For all the latest titles coming soon,
visit millsandboon.co.uk/nextmonth